Walking Bloody Paper Dolls

Could the murdered kill his murderer in the end?

Author LiaoHong Sun

Translators Bin Liu & Jirong Liu

WALKING BLOODY PAPER DOLLS

First edition. February 2, 2024.

ISBN: 979-8224460755

Written by LiaoHong Sun.

Chapter 1 The murdered killed the murderer in the end

Ah! How could it happen in that fashion, it was too mysterious, it was really unbelievable!

The thing happened in middle of September in lunar calendar. There was a well-known Buddhist society which was holding a small scale lecture about the classic sutra. The lecture did not focus its attention on a whole book of a sutra, everyday the speaking monk would choose a subject he liked to explain some tenets of Buddhism. The lecture would only last for ten days. There was a particular term for such a kind of lecture: Discovery.

In the day it was fifth day of the lecture.

According to routine, the presiding monk introduced the speaker while holding an incense in his hands to announce the beginning of the lecture. Lay Buddhists in the room began to stand up, followed the presiding monk to sing psalm of a burning incense will make the whole world have sweet fragrance, ended the singing with 'my master Sakyamuni Buddha'. Gentle smoke was rising in the burner in front of the podium, peaceful sounds of knocking wooden fish could be heard in the room, the solemn air was spreading out of the room and into the world. Though the lecture was not huge, it was quite solemn, if someone was holding something which was unmentionable to other in the room, he would feel apprehensive in his heart.

At the end of the singing, the speaking monk began to give his lecture while drooping his eyebrows and adopting a sitting position with double crossed legs as a Buddha, he knocked his ruler gently to announce the beginning of his lecture.

The name of the speaking monk was SnowyNature, he was not very old, but he was already a merciful and well-known master of the school which holds all Buddhisms has same meaning. In the day he did not talk about the essential concepts such as everything and every idea was germinated in one's mind, everything existed in a way as one thought, the thing did not have its own good or bad nature, only one's thinking gave it a meaning of good or bad etc. He just chose a simple term Karma which everyone knew the term very well, tried to explain in a simple language about the meaning of the word to a Buddhist.

He said:" In universe Karma is the most essential law. The cause-effect relationship of Karma acts like a host and its shadow. There is no independent shadow in the world, there is no host without of its shadow. Furthermore, what a kind of form decides what a kind of shadow which would show up. For example, in front of a mirror, when one is smiling, in the mirror it will definitely not show up an angry expression; when one is staring, in the mirror it will definitely not show up a smiling expression. Therefore, for all people, you will get a good effect if you do something good as a cause; you will get a bad effect if you do something bad as a cause, none could get anything which will violate the law. Based on the law, if an individual curses and hits a man, then the individual will definitely be cursed and hit by other people; if an individual kills a man, then the individual could not escape the fate he will be killed by other people!"

"Nevertheless, Buddha said: ' A sin starts from one's thinking, a sin ends from one's thinking. So long as one could control one's thinking, anything would come and go at once.' Therefore, for anyone who committed a sin, so long as the one really wants to repent sincerely, then the effect might be transferred away or changed to another one."

Those were the essentials of the lecture in the day.

In the day, besides the essentials, Master SnowyNature gave several believable examples to demonstrate the truthfulness of his words. He spoke fluently with his calm and sincere expression and voice. His audience was enchanted by the lecture as if there were listening a legendary story, thus his words moved those believers of the audiences, even those who did not have a strong belief could not help but think and believe Buddhism in their hearts.

Among the lay monks, there was a special guest, who was received by a particular staff of the society, based on the hospitable expression of the staff, one could guess the lofty position of the guest in society.

The guest was with a noble expression, a blue gown and a black vest. He was about over fifty years age. He had a melon seed type face with a broad forehead, wide and tall cheekbones and a tapered chin. His eyes were small piercing ones with many wrinkles at the corners of his eyes. He had a bearing of skilled calculation for everything. When he raised his hand, his fingers of left hand adopted a grasping position for a cigar, furthermore, there was a sparkling huge diamond ring on his index finger, which was a great stimulus to those poor believers of Buddhism.

The rich gentleman was a 'well-known' person in the financial circle of the city. He was a powerful man in the circle. Recently he did several excellent performances in cornering the market for food of people, which achieved quite a good result. Thus, anyone who had lived for some time in the city, when they heard his name BrilliantTalent Wang, they could not help but admire him greatly.

For recent one to two months, this 'well-known' person, probably he spent too much about his mind, developed an extremely unhealthy problem. In comparison with the poor, the rich paid a high attention to their body: So long as they had three sneezes, they had to visit a doctor to find what's wrong with their body. Based on the diagnosis: He overspent his mind and energy, needs to have a good rest to get his body recovered to former good status. If he does not, he might develop hysteria. The diagnosis was really a threat to the rich people like him. Thus he had to follow the advice of the doctor to leave all the things at his hand behind his back and to have a good rest for the time being.

As he was in his resting period, once when he had a chat with his friends, he heard they talked about the lecture of the monks. In the day, as he was quite happy, thus he came to the temple to have his first happiness to accompany Buddha. He did not know much about Buddhism before. Unexpectedly, after he heard the lecture, he was greatly moved, particularly about the words from the speaking monk, the words were forced down into his mind like a nail, the words definitely could not be erased no matter.

Though the thing mentioned above was very coarse on its appearance, in fact it seemed the description had already gone into a detail. As it became a simple reason which would draw up a formless curtain about a weird and mysterious story; the mystery about the story was beyond the imagination of a human.

Chapter 2 He Strangled His Enemies Who Framed Him Up To Death After Climbing Out His Grave

After the lecture, BrilliantTalent Wang had an unmentionable worry, there was a severe melancholy expression on his face, his manner and voice often showed a bit in trance status. Usually he was a steadfast and calm man, no matter how severe a thing was, the thing would not affect his calmness. Thus his abnormal expression could be easily noticed by people around him.

His wife—PendantJade—was a kind and gentle woman. She was almost half of his age. They met each other in a whorehouse. Though the woman had a background as a prostitute, she did not get much the habit of a prostitute. The reason was: She was born in a very good family in a remote countryside, due to some accident, she was pushed into the fire pit of the city. Thus, after she got married, she still kept the gentle and considerate manner of a woman from a good family to her husband.

As he often fell into in trance, which made the young wife feel quite apprehensive. She asked him several times what's wrong, why he acted in such a kind of uneasy manner. But our well-known man denied anything was wrong even to his most intimate wife.

Fortunately, after several days, it seemed that his abnormal status returned normal. After several more days, the melancholy expression vanished from his face. But even a tiny stone dropped into a peaceful surface of a lake, it would cause many ripples. His uneasy mind after the lecture was just first ripple after a dropping stone into the lake of his mind, there was second ripple, and more ripples would come out of the dropping stone and would spread out further and further outward.

The expanding of second ripple happened as following:

In the day, after he finished his lunch, he was sitting in a cushioned chair and reading a piece of newspaper easily and comfortably. There was a piece of advertisement in the newspaper drawing his attention at once, that was a film ad for Grand Bright Theatre. In first place, there was a new film showing in the theatre, the film was called *Revenge After Reincarnation*. There were following ad words for the film:

He strangled his enemies who framed him up to death after climbing out his grave!

It was quite normal for a film ad to use some eye-popping words to draw an attention of potential moviegoers. To a normal reader, the ad was quite unique, which might arouse his interest to go to the theatre to watch the movie. But as soon as the words entered his view, the words made his heart shiver with coldness and jump rapidly and forcibly! At the same time, the words he heard in the lecture several days ago began to echo in his ears, it seemed that the speaking monk earnestly said to his ear:

—If you killed someone, in the end, you will be killed by someone as your effect for your cause!—-

At the same time, the melancholy expression several days ago showed up again on his face. He was beset by the ordinary ad for a film in an uncontrollable fashion.

There was a common and interesting psychological reaction: the more one is afraid of one thing, the more one would focus his attention on the thing. For example, if one is afraid of ghost, he sleeps alone in a house, in midnight he will feel more horrible in the house, then he will focus his attention more on everything in the house. At the moment, he had fallen into such a kind of status, thus the first thing was he wanted to go to see the film, what kind of plot the film would have? In a blink, he would deny his thinking: No, it is unnecessary to see the film. As the doctor told him: In the period of your rest and recovery, it is inappropriate to get strong stimulus to your mind.

Should he go or not? The two ideas began to fight a delicate war in his mind. He checked the clock on the wall several times within several minutes, as the next movie would be due in a short time. But no matter what kind of decision he would make, he could not sit in his cushioned chair calmly and comfortably anymore. In the end, he stood up suddenly, came out of the room, told his driver:"Get the car for me, now!"

Usually this well-known man did not like to see a film, it was quite exceptional for him to go to the cinema. In a short time the car arrived at the front of the theatre, the driver with his surprised look watched his host walking into the theatre hurriedly. Five minutes later, the well-known man had already sat in a chair in the theatre, in a short while, the white screen began to show the film.

Revenge After Reincarnation, what was the film about? Maybe some readers had already watched the film, as the film was related to this novel, thus it was necessary to introduce the plot of the film briefly here: The main role of the film was played by Kavrov, the most famous actor for playing horror films. An unemployed man was framed up as a murderer by five rascals. As the frame-up was carefully designed and implemented, the innocent man could not exculpate himself from the crime as he could not provide any evidence for his innocence, thus he was given a death sentence with no reason.

An old doctor knew the man was innocent, he came forward to rescue and exculpate the man, but the rascals tried to obstruct his action, thus his rescuing action was delayed considerably. In the end, when the doctor went to the execution room, the pitiable man was already electrocuted in a bed, thus he became a wronged ghost.

The angry doctor took the corpse of the man into his laboratory, tried best with all his efforts, saved the dead man, took him back from the hand of the god of death, gave him a new life with a new scientific technology.

The pitiable man changed to another man in his personality after his rebirth. What strange was that: Before he was electrocuted, he did not know anything about the men who framed him up. But after he got his rebirth, based on a mysterious power, he could recognize the five rascals clearly. In the end, he strangled each of them to death by himself, then committed a suicide, thus went back again to the embrace of the god of death.

That was the synopsis of the story. The film was a popular horror movie at the moment.

Though the movie was a horror film, it was much better to describe it as a shocking tragedy. There were two scenes which moved its audiences most, including: first, when the unemployed one came out of his cell and was about to send to the electrocution chair, he raised his head, shouted miserably to the sky:' Ah! God! Only you—believe me!' Though the script was very short, his voice was filled with anger and despair, his expression was so melancholy, helpless and sad, his voice was accompanied by the sad sound of a violin and the dim background of the prison, which made every audience could not help but get a tense and sharp feeling in his every nerve as if his nerve were pricked by a needle; second, after he got his rebirth, in a concert, he bumped into the rascals who framed him up. At the moment he surveyed alternately the enemies with his cold gaze, under the close-up shot his eyes was filled with the most sharp and hateful look in the world, the eyes emanated the hateful look at his enemies! Thus not only the rascals on the screen but also the audiences in dark showed an intense expression on their faces.

In a word, the film did satisfy the curiosity of its audiences, but to the writer, the one who got the stimulus most was the protagonist of this novel BrilliantTalent Wang!

Chapter 3 A Pair Of Angry Eyes Which Were More Malevolent Than Those of Kavlov Staring At Him

The film came to an end, the climaxes on the screen died out one after another. The tense nerves gradually recovered to their calmness. Only in the mind of BrilliantTalent Want, billowy waves began to rush forward. He was rushed out of the theatre in the wave, felt weak in his legs, staggered forward as if he were drunken. When he stepped into the bright street, he felt a bit darkness in his eyes. If the driver had not call him, he might not be able to find his own car.

My goodness! The film left him a profound impression! He still remembered the two ferocious and hateful eyes of the protagonist, the eyes were extremely flashing in front of his eyes whether he closed or opened his eyes. It could be put in such a way, the image might not be able to leave his memory even after he died. My goodness, was his acting skill so superb? No! The impression he held in his memory was not completely related to the skill of the actor, to be more specific, there were a pair of angry eyes which were more malevolently staring at him in his mind than those of the actor!

Inside the car on his way back to his home, a memory was flashing back into his mind which was his most horrible and painful experience happened twelve years ago.

Twelve years ago, he was not the man with huge wealth in front of us at the moment. At that time he was a poor guy. His former name was IntelligentOne Wang, he lived in a remote town in Zhejiang Province, the town was about ten kilometers away from the county town of Sheng County which was haunted by armed bandits frequently. Though the town was a small place, it was located in the way to ShaoXing from Sheng County, thus in the small town there was a small hostel with very simple facility. The hostel had a beautiful name, Spring Flower. At that time, he worked as a factotum, though he was called a factotum, in fact besides the owner, he played roles of a manager, a cashier, a receptionist, a chef and other things. Therefore he was an important person to the hostel. People living in the town all knew him as he was very famous in the town.

He was known for his cleverness and vigilance in the town, due to his cleverness and vigilance he painted a bloody painting by himself later.

The thing happened in a cold, miserable, windy rain night. It was in the middle of September of lunar calendar at that time. In comparison with city, after supper, the town was enshrouded into a lonely and quiet atmosphere. The lamp under the eave of the hostel was swaying in the night screen weaved by rain. When one looked from faraway, it was a miserable yellow halo as if the lamp were about to fall into sleep or it might go off in a moment. In the hostel, the owner and IntelligentOne Wang were about to get ready to close the gate, suddenly a man hurriedly entered the hostel for a night stay.

The man held an oil paper umbrella, took a small cloth package, looked like a coolie from countryside. He had a worn-out thick pelt hat on his head, the rim of the hat almost reached his eyebrows,—at the moment, he needed not to wear that kind of thick hat according to season—, he wore a dirty black cotton padded jacket, along the shoulders there were some broken places of the jacket. He had a working apron around his waist. He wore a pair of straw sandals covered with mud. It was quite obvious that he had already walked a long way to reach the hostel.

The man said his name was NinthOne Tao, came from the county town of Sheng County, would visit his relative in ShaoXing City, passed through the town, wanted to have a clean and quiet single room to stay for several days by himself.

"My goodness! With such a kind of manner, he wants to have a clean and quiet single room!" The owner looked at the customer with a blank expression, said to himself in his heart, and could not help but show a surprising expression at the corners of his eyes. The guest understood the meaning of the owner very well, immediately he took out some money from the pocket of his broken jacket, handed it to the owner, said 'the advance for room and food for several days."

The guest handed the owner five shiny silver coins, which made the hand of the owner tremble a bit, because none of his customer before had given him such a large amount of money for one time. At the moment, of course he satisfied the requirement of his customer willingly and obediently.

But at the moment IntelligentOne Wang was watching at the side, a doubt was arising in his vigilant mind. He thought as this man just passed through the hostel on his way to another place, he should just stay for one night and leave for his destination in next day, why he wanted to pay advances for several days? When the man handed his money, his hand was very clean and fair with a long nail in his little finger, which was different with the his apparels; why he wanted to have a single quiet and remote room?"

As he had several doubts about the guest, he could not help but survey the guest carefully. Based on his estimate, the age of the guest was between forty to fifty. Under the lamplight, the guest looked pale and apprehensive. There were two quite obvious marks on the face of the guest: a red pea sized black mole with several hairs about one inch in length on his left ear; three deep wrinkles in the center between his eyebrows, the central one was long, the ones around it were shorter, thus the wrinkles formed a bit aslant steel-fork-like pattern. For a moment, if one looked at the steel-fork-like wrinkles with a murderous air, the wrinkles looked quite deep, which left quite an impression which could not be forgotten easily.

In the night, the guest, NinthOne Tao as he called himself, was led to a clean, quiet and single room. At the guest paid quite a sum, which made the important clerk of the hostel, IntelligentOne Wang, had to offer special treatment to him. When the guest was about to enter the room, he hospitably offered his hand to take the cloth package of the guest, thus he could send the package to the room. Unexpectedly, his hospitable action was declined unkindly. At the moment, the steel-fork-like wrinkles of the guest went deeper again, simultaneously, his hand had already touched the package and felt it was a bit heavy.

The little act made him cannot help but doubt even more strongly. Based on his careful observations, he thought the guest was a bit mysterious, particularly the package increased the mysterious even more.

Then what was inside the important package?

At last under secret observation in dark, a novel finding was showed up.

Chapter 4 Walking Paper Doll From White Paper

It was very late in night, the lamp in the room of the guest was still on. Outside of the room, IntelligentOne Wang was peeping into the room with his held breath through the window. Of course you should know the window was not the glass window with steel frame like one was very popular in Shanghai with brocade curtain; the window was just a kind of paper window which was very popular in nineteenth century, which was very easy to do surveillance of the room from outside through the window.

In such a melancholy rain night, what he was doing in the room at such a late hour?

IntelligentOne Wang looked through the slit of the window, at once, he was stupefied by what he saw.

In the first place, the guest was unpacking his cloth package under the dim kerosene lamp light and counting the things inside the package solemnly. There were two to three broken clothes at the bottom of the package, several piles of paper money. It should be at least several hundreds? No, at least near one thousand or more. In addition, there were several paper rolls, though numbers were not many, they were heavy, then they must be silver coins! The last one was wrapped in a very thick paper, my goodness, all were gold jewelries! The jewelries were shining under the dim light.

My goodness! In the dark night, with the blue lamp shade, the room was dim, on the broken table, gold was shiny yellow, silver was shiny white, paper money was colorful, the combined various colors turned the peeping eyes into greedy red ones through reflection.

IntelligentOne Wang let himself calm down, noticed the mysterious guy in the room creeping down under the bed, put the wealth at a remote corner under the bed which was not easy to notice, then stood up, dusted the dirt on his knees away, then refolded the old clothes into a package and put at the side of his pillow.

IntelligentOne Wang stood quietly in dark with his widely opened eyes as if he were in dream. It's a pity, since he came to the world till the moment, in his narrow small eyes which looked like the ones of a mice, he had never seen so much wealth! Fortunately, in the night his curiosity was completely satisfied with the witness of the huge wealth through sacrificing his sleep. But under that kind of condition, it seemed that it was not enough by just looking, there was a hungry feeling welling out of the bottom of his heart.

Thus, in dark a smart brain began to think further rapidly about the thing.

"For a man with his appearance, how could he have so much wealth with him? This guy should not be a good guy, right?" That was the first idea flashing into his mind in dark.

"Why he hided his thing under the bed in such haste fashion? At least he should not come here to choose this room as his storage room from a faraway place, right? Yes! Understood! He must keep a vigilance on me. Because before he entered the room, I gave a particular attention to his package. Yes! He must think in such fashion!" That was the second idea coming out of his clever mind.

"The thing under the bed, except me, none else knows a bit. In case, the guy dies of acute illness! Then, I—-how wonderful..." That was the third idea coming out of his wild thinking from his intelligent mind.

"But the king of the hell is not my brother-in-law, why he would take my order—-" That was his fifth idea, then he thought from another angle," then, do I have a way to implement the responsibility of the king of the hell?"

"My goodness! No! It's a sin!" His sixth idea enjoined him stopping his wishful thinking; but the last idea turned rapidly in another direction:"Humph! The guy is not a nice man. Maybe, he is a robber. The thing in his package came from his robbery and murder. As it is the wealth from unjust action, everyone could take it way, what are you hesitating for?"

His mind turned rapidly like the colorful pictures in a cartoon film as if it were a swirling windmill.

Anyway, a smart man always could come out a smart decision. After a period of wild thinking, in his intelligent mind, he suddenly recalled an incident had happened in the town.

Not a long time ago, in the town, there was a weird incident. In the first place, several children were kidnapped away. Such a kind of thing had never happened in the remote and small town before, what even more as a coincidence, in next day after the incidence, the only son about eight years old of the most powerful man in the town fell into acute illness suddenly, cried for his abdominal pain, died in the night. The two things were no related at all in any aspect, but for people living in remote place, they had only simple thinking, they united the things together and thought from a united angle, thus they developed a rumor which was not only weird but also unreasonable—maybe they were under heavily influence of so called novels of martial arts—which was spreading widely and rapidly in the town, people in the town said there were some remnant member of White Lotus Society who came to the town and particularly snatched children. If they could snatch a child away, that should be fine; if they could not snatch a child away, they would cast a spell to take the heart or liver of the child away to make medicine or some magic things. As soon as the rumor was spreading in the small town, everyone in the town was frightened, to them it seemed that the disaster would fall on their heads at once. At the moment, the powerful man who had lost his only son, besides his sadness and anger, offered a five hundred silver coins award to catch the sorcerer in the rumor. Needless to day, none could not catch even the wind or shadow left behind him.

The incident happened in less than three month ago. At the moment, though the incident was over, people with children in the town were still frightened with the loss of the color of their face if someone occasionally mentioned about the thing. Of course, the powerful man was still with the pain of the loss of his only son.

IntelligentOne Wang recalled the incident, in dark, his mind flashed brightly once. He peeped through a slit of the window for a last glance, suddenly an idea came into his mind.

In the night he returned to his living place, he slept in his bed and planned for quite a while.

In next day, he took a chance when the guest left his room, sneaked into the room, set up an ingenious trap. In the evening, he ran to the mansion of the the powerful, reported the following thing to the man while gasping for his breath.

He said:" Sir, I have to report to you, the sorcerer of White Lotus Society comes to our town again! He is living in our hostel. He is a man with evil looking, there is a mole on his left ear, three deep wrinkles between his eyebrows; he arrived in last night; my goodness! It's horrible! I saw he was preparing a lot of paper dolls from white paper under lamp, the dolls could walk by themselves! If you don't believe me, you just go to check by yourself!"

The news was a complete surprise to the listeners, everyone was shocked and troubled by the information. Though there was no telephone at that time in the town, the information acted like a hurricane, blew all over the town. In less than half an hour, a lot of people came to the outside of the hostel, the wave of human rushed into the room of the guest with the head of village security as a leader, the shocking and surprising situation frightened the owner and his wife, which surprised the guest called NinthOne Tao even more greatly, he was transfixed as he did not know what kind of nightmare he could face out of the thing. He thought some misunderstanding had happened, for his own safety, he could only run away in his mind. While he was flustered with an action of preparing to run away, his manner enforced the idea of the people that he was guilty, as a result, under the fist and feet of the people, he was tied up tightly. Then under the watch of the people, someone found three paper dolls of white paper in his small package. In addition, there was a piece of small red paper with birth dates of several children, including the one of the only son of the powerful.

My goodness! He was the sorcerer who would take the heart and liver of a child away from White Lotus Society, with such a kind of evidence, how could he prove his innocence to exculpate himself.

At the period it was lawless dark times, due to the roaring anger, most importantly, due to the firing anger of the powerful for the loss of his only son, at the moment the man did not get any due trial process, as a result, he even did not have a chance to prove his own innocence, he was to be executed to cut his heart out by the order of the powerful man who actually acted as a local tyrant, thus he would die without his awareness what's wrong with himself.

Chapter 5 My Good Heaven! Please Tell Me What's My Crime?

In next morning, a bloody scene would show up at once in front of the people:

The morning was a dull one with a livid sky liked the face of the condemned. In a bleak and remote place, the condemned was with his bared upper body, knelt down in the ground, his hands were tied back on a wooden column. There were three mysterious paper dolls plus a yellow magic figure attached in front of his chest, the yellow magic figure was from an old Taoist monk in the town, he said:"It's true. The little paper dolls are alive! If they are not suppressed by a magic spell, they won't die together with their owner, they would act as ghosts to avenge their owner!" The words increased the horrible and mysterious atmosphere of the incident.

Several steps away from the front of the condemned, there was a white table, there was a tablet of the dead son of the powerful man set on the center of the table, the tablets of the missing children were invited to sit around the tablet by honor. The table was covered with dedicated vegetables, rice, and paper money in a form of silver. Two lighted red candles were trembling in wind while dropping blood-like tears, which symbolized the short-life span of the murdered. The most conspicuous thing on the table was a wooden plate with a shiny sharp double-edged knife!

In the first place, they were planning to gorge out the heart of a live man in a cruel and inhuman way!

Almost all the people of the town came to the remote and desolate place, the people formed a wall of human bodies around the place. Some wore angry expression, some tense, some expectant. Most of them held a feeling to watch a play, a live play they had not watched never before. The important person of the hostel IntelligentOne Wang was also one of the standers-by watching the free show.

Just at the moment when the cruel show was about to play, the condemned stared his eyes widely open as if he just woke up from his sleep, looked at the the wooden plate and the shiny knife, knew what he was about to face, trembled with fear, shouted sorrowfully to the sky with his pallid face:

"Good Heaven! Please tell me, what's my crime? In my home I have an old mother, a wife and son, and..." He choked due to his sob, he could not speak anything more due to his fear.

Among the standing people, some began to curse, some began to throw stone and broken tiles to him, some began to spit at him, but none showed any sympathy to him.

With one exception, IntelligentOne Wang turned his face slightly to another direction with his merciful heart.

"If, there is a karma in this world—" the condemned began to shout with his last energy at the end of his life as if it was the last flame of his life, the steel-fork-like wrinkles between his eyebrows appeared even deeper, he said through his clenched teeth:" The one who demands my death will get even more cruel effect than I! Though I will die, my vengeful ghost will climb out of my grave in daytime, I will find my enemy and claim his life!"

At the last moment when he ended his promise of avenging his own death, his eyes became two flammable hot balls; his tears due to the injustice had already dried. He scanned each of the audiences standing around with his cold and hateful look like the one of a viper gradually, steadfastly, in the end, he focused his look on IntelligentOne Wang—Whether the condemned did it intentionally or accidentally, none was sure, right? But in his heart, IntelligentOne Wang thought the condemned had focused the most hateful and malevolent gaze on him, the eyes focused the emanating light on him!

At the moment, there was a dark and melancholy seed buried deep into the mind of IntelligentOne Wang! The seed had been germinating and harassing him till his death, even at the last moment of his life it was still acting in his mind.

In one moment at the time, the face of IntelligentOne Wang looked as horrible as the condemned. But anyway, he was a great intelligent well-known person, thus in next moment his face returned to its normal color, furthermore, in order to show his calmness and steadfastness, he stood to watch at the scene leisurely till the end.

He watched the makeshift executioner—a butcher in the town—pierced the knife into the heart of the condemned, an angry blood flow gushed out of the chest of the condemned, the blood stained the paper dolls in his chest into bloody ones at once, horrible bloody dolls!

A barbarian live show ended among the bustling people. But was the executed one a member who gorged out liver and heart of a child of White Lotus Society?

The answer was no, absolutely not! He did not have anything to do with White Lotus Society, even in his dream. Though he looked like a bad man with his appearance, in fact he was a good man who knew how to behave himself in his life, just a bit rich man outside the county town of Sheng County, his real name was BrightSpring Kuang. He owned dozens acres of crop fields and dozens thousands money, though the amount was not that huge, but in his hometown, he was a well-known man with a plenty cash in his hand. Thus he became a focus of a group of bandits who migrated around his area. He got a letter from the head of the bandits, told him to prepare a hundred thousand dollars as soon as possible, handed the money to them as pay for soldiers, if he could not accomplish the demand, he would be treated with a cruel method beyond his imagination! The head of the bandits was well known for his cruelty, he would do what he said he would do as he had already set several horrible examples before. The threatening letter was equal to a death sentence to the man with some wealth. At that chaotic time, none could easily differentiate between soldiers and bandits, he could not get normal protection from related institutions. If he agreed the demand, he really could not find that much money; if he did not, he could not escape the evil hand of the bandits. Thus he had only one option, ran away with his home and land left behind him for his own life. He had five members in his family, his old mother, wife, a son about thirty years and a daughter about fifteen. They discussed that if they all ran away together, they might not be able to escape from the surveillance of the bandits, thus he ran away first after he dressed himself up. Before he left, his wife packed all their money into a small package, took a chance of melancholy and rainy night, ran away from the surveillance of the bandits with a broken oil paper umbrella apprehensively. He knew there was a small hostel more than 10 kilometers away in a small town from his home, he told his family members that he would wait them in the hostel, after they gathered together, they would run to ShaoXing or Hangzhou as a whole family.

Unfortunately, due to his money, he just escaped from the hand of the bandits and fell into a death trap set up for him by another man. Wasn't it a powerful evidence to the one who believed in fatalism?

The truth behind the thing was gradually known to the people of the town. In next several days, the crying sound of the mother, the wife and the son and the daughter of the condemned reached into the ears of the people in the town. At the moment the smart IntelligentOne Wang had already vanished from the town and run to other place, and did not tell anyone where he would go.

The future well-known man of the town held a bit of anger before he left the town as the powerful man of the town broke his promise for five hundred dollars of award. He thought if he had not gotten the wealth hidden under the bed, a life would be wasted for nothing! But when he recovered the money hidden under the bed which should be taken as stained with blood, he was surprised by the amount of the wealth, took the money as a reward to kill the one by the hands of the others, the total amount for the paper money was nine thousand four hundred and fifty dollars; plus the silver coins and gold jewelries, he estimated the total amount was over thirteen thousands. Thus he became a rich man in such an easy fashion.

In September of the year, he sneaked into Shanghai, at the same time, he became a gentle BrilliantTalent Wang from a despicable IntelligentOne Wang at once.

Thus after short twelve years, based on his intelligence and vigilance, he had already become a well-known person in Shanghai.

Chapter 6 My goodness! He Was The Condemned Sorcerer Of White Lotus Society Executed Twelve Years Ago!

BrilliantTalent Wang came out the theatre, huddled up at the corner of the car, though the gaze of his eyes had already left the screen a long while ago, there was an invisible screen popped up in his mind. The extremely horrible and cruel scene twelve years ago replayed in his mind clearly. When he returned to his home, as soon as he recalled the look of Kavrov, he would associate the look with the eyes in his memory which had same look as Kavrov: He only sensed the pair of eyes which were as evil and cruel and malevolent as the ones of a viper were piercing at him from every direction of the room!

The melancholy expression in his face worsened further.

He regretted greatly that he should not go to watch the horrible film, which lead to his horror for no reason. Nevertheless, the horror could not only be ascribed to the movie. In fact, there was another weird incident which was the real cause of his uneasiness.

The incident happened several days ago before he went to the lecture of the Buddhist society. It was a bright sunny day. He just got back from his business trip, when he got out of his car, suddenly a middle aged man passed by his shoulder. Just with a glance, he thought the man was with a very familiar face, as if they saw each other quite often. But to his own strangeness, he just could not remember where he had seen the man before, who was the man? When he returned his home, he remembered the man at once. My goodness! He was none else but the executed sorcerer of White Lotus Society by cutting his heart out! The more he tried to recall his face, the more the man looked like the executed one! The more he thought, the more his blood was boiling, it seemed that all his blood flow came to a halt.

He became quite apprehensive, sensed something horrible might befall on his head at any moment.

But after all he was a calm and steadfast man. After thinking further, he thought his thinking was naive and ridiculous. How could the world have a ghost? Even if the world is with a ghost , how could he come here to avenge his own death? If a ghost could claim someone's life, why should the ghost wait for twelve years to do that? Furthermore, he met the man in bright day, the man must look similar to the one executed, plus he had his own apprehensive suspicion, which led to such a kind of illusion. Yes, it must happen in such fashion!

After such a kind of self-explanation, he felt quite easy. If without other stimuli, he might have already forgotten the thing completely. Unfortunately, several days later he went to the society for the lecture, the presiding monk even said the following words:

"if an individual kills a man, then the individual could not escape the fate he will be killed by other people!"

Then, he happened to go to the movie to see the film with the weird line:

"He strangled his enemies who framed him up to death after climbing out his grave!"

The above words made him recall the horrible swear from the condemned before he was killed, he swore angrily:

"If there is a Karma in this world, the one who demands my death will get even more cruel effect than I! Though I will die, my vengeful ghost will climb out of my grave in daytime, I will find my enemy and claim his life!"

As he recalled the horrible swear, he could not help but recall the man he came across in front of his house. My goodness! Did I really bump into a ghost? The more he thought about the thing, the more he became scared, it was a kind of unnameable tremor, as if a viper had sneaked into this heart. From then on, he would become frightened for no reason; when he was sitting alone by himself, he would see a fleeting black shadow across his eyes. Under such a kind of condition, his nerves were tortured frequently. Though he continuously consoled himself with the words 'there is no ghost in the world', his heart did not want to accept the comforting words anymore.

In first place a suspicion would produce a ghost which was beyond doubt, what he came across had some solid basis which was not completely from his own imagination. Therefore an extremely horrible and unbelievable thing showed up in front him clearly and truly.

The horrible thing happened in the day, what coincidental was the day was 'black Friday' to those superstitious men in west. It was around dusk when he came back to his home from outside. The dim dusk light had already enshrouded the house.

Recently due to the darkness in his heart, the well-known man yearned for the outside brightness, furthermore, he had a very bad temper, he would fly into rage for just a tiny thing. When he entered the house, he noticed the light was not on, he had already became angry. He climbed up the staircases hurriedly with his lowered head, after five to six steps as he was just in the middle of staircases, he raised his head once, noticed a man coming down the staircases with a black hat with a broad rim and a black cloth gown and a cloth package under his arm. At the moment he transferred his anger to the man from his servant who did not turn on the lights, he was about to shout:"Who are you, why you come up to the upstairs without being invited!"

Before he opened his mouth, he suddenly noticed the feature of the man, felt at once his body was covered with goose bumps, all hairs in his body stood up as straightly as possible!

In the first place at the end of the passageway, at the left side a door was open—the door was the one of his bedroom—light from the electric lamplight of the room shone on the face on the man at the entrance of the staircases from side, which made the feature of the man could be clearly watched. Under the intermingled light of the setting glow and the lamplight, the face of the man was as pallid as a dead man without a bit redness, as if his face were painted heavily with lime white. The familiar and horrible face was the one he dreamed often in his sleep recently! Particularly the grim eyes were shooting cold blue light at him as if the light were from a viper!

The situation persisted for a blink. What strange was that when the man saw him, the man was with a fearful expression, the man dodged to left at once silently, then vanished like a wisp of a smoke in a wink.

But in the period of a blink, BrilliantTalent Wang—without any possibility of making a mistake—saw clearly the man was the one he came across several days ago in front of his house, to be more specific, the man was the executed one who died of being cut out of his heart twelve years ago. Really! He kept his promise of that time, he really crawled out of his grave!

The lungs of BrilliantTalent Wang fanned very hard and rapidly, it seemed that his whole body dropped into an ice hole, cold sweats came out of every pore of his body, his underclothes attached to his body due to the sweats. At the moment due to the strength he was not aware, his paralyzed body still stood at the half way of the staircases without rolling down the staircases.

It seemed that his feet were nailed down on the staircases tightly. For quite a long time he did not know—in fact it was just a moment—he noticed another black shadow at the entrance of the staircases, his heart jumped quickly once again, he looked at the figure carefully, she was his wife, PendantJade.

The woman looked down at the staircases, shouted surprisingly:

"My goodness! BrilliantTalent! You, what's wrong with you?" She hurriedly came down to half the way of the staircases, supported him, and pulled him to upstairs with a great effort. She felt his hand was ice-cold and his body was trembling.

When he entered the bedroom, he calmed down a bit. His wife thought he fell into sudden illness, but he declined categorically, just said he felt a bit comfortable, urged his wife to turn on all the lights of the house.

The young woman followed his order, looked at him apprehensively, felt rather baffled.

Usually he did not like to drink, but in the night with persuasion of his considerate and gentle wife, he drank a lot of wine to get himself drunk. After he became drunk, he began to ramble incoherently, which frightened and perplexed his wife dearly for whole night.

From the day on, our well-known man could not maintain his calmness. If we copied a sentence from some philosopher to describe his change, then he had already changed from a quantitative aspect to a qualitative one suddenly.

Chapter 7 One Leg Of The Paper Doll Was Squeezed Under The Window In A Position As If It Wanted To Force Into The Room !

After he bumped into the horrible ghost, for several days, fortunately nothing happened. BrilliantTalent Wang felt a bit relaxed in his heart. Of course none could say that the whirlpool in his heart came to a complete stop, it would not expand in any direction anymore.

Several days later, he was sitting at a desk to read a book in his living room to while away his boring time. During the quietness, suddenly he smelled a kind of stinky smell of burning cloth. According to custom: For any place to have such a kind of smell, it means the place is being haunted by a ghost. But at that time he did not think in such a direction, just put down his book, tried to locate the source of the smell. He raised his eyes, suddenly noticed there was a white thing at the bottom between the two panels of the window, the white thing was waving in wind. He stood up from his chair, noticed it was a paper doll, one leg was squeezed under the window in a position as if it wanted to squeezed into the room.

The little thing almost made him stop his breathing completely! Fortunately it was in daytime. He took the thing into his trembling hand while mustering up his courage, noticed: The paper was about three inches in length. The paper-cut silhouette was vivid with its muscular buttocks, furthermore the face was a painted one with eyes, noses, mouth and ears. Though the drawing was very simple, the bulging and staring eyes looked like live ones; what more horrible was that the face was just a miniature of the face of one who died of being cut out of his heart twelve years ago!

There were three thin lines between eyebrows of the paper doll, which represented the horrible steel-fork-like wrinkles; there was a dot as large as if it was pierced by a needle on its left ear, which represented the black mole. There were many red spots of various sizes in front of the chest, which was not painted by red ink or paint, it seemed that they were real bloodstains, and the blood would drop down from there to ground. Furthermore, there was a little sharp knife holding tightly in the right hand of the thing.

For unknown reason, fear and apprehension filled into every cell of his body. He jumped due to a disgusting feeling, threw the horrible thing into the furnace angrily.

The paper doll was threw onto a piece of burning coal, it did not turn into flame at once. The hard and endurable paper contracted due to the hotness. He noticed the upper part of the doll stood up angrily and horribly in the flame, it seemed that the little arm with the knife contracted and raised gradually as if it wanted to lunge forward.

At the same time, the air was filled with a specific smell of burning bloody cloth, the smell was floating around his nose.

He stretched his hand to caress his head, wanted to leave the tense atmosphere at once, rushed to the door in a confused status, took the handle in his hand, just pulled the door open to a slit, in his flustered status, he heard a gasping breathing sound, which directly pierced onto the eardrums, the sound stopped his action of opening the door, he paused for a moment, then pulled the door open suddenly, found nothing was there through the door.

Of course, the weird situation enhanced his terror further. After tremble for a while, he thought his body was growing uncontrollably.

But the weird incident developed more and more strangely.

In next day, a guest came to the house of the well-known man. The guest was tall with square shoulders, there was a lively air between his eyebrows. He was a student of business to IntelligentTalent Wang, about thirty years old with a modern manner. At the same time he was a frequent visitor, thus he would come and go at anytime as he liked as if the place were his own house. His name was MiddleHero Qiu, everyone in the house called him Little Qiu.

In the day he came to the house to deliver a business contract.

As the contract was very important, when he got the contract, he wanted to put the contract into his safe box at once. He went hurriedly up to upstairs, as soon as he opened the safe box, suddenly, he stared with his widely opened eyes and lost his mind in trance for a moment.

In the first place, he smelled the same burning cloth smell again. He let himself calm down a bit, turned back and noticed Little Qiu standing behind him, did not want Little Qiu notice his worrying and frightening expression. Therefore, he pretended to be calm and acted as if nothing were wrong, but when he stretched his hand to put the contract into his safe box, his face became even more pale, furthermore, his upset expression immediately reflected on the face of Little Qiu.

"What's wrong? Sir!" the youth asked in a caring and worrying tone.

"It has nothing to do with you! I just feel a bit faint," while answering the question, he waved his hand to the young man, said:"You wait me at downstairs, you need not to stand here."

The anxious expression and tone was absolutely abnormal. The youth could only follow his order bewilderingly and haltingly. Little Qiu just turned his body and was about to leave the room, then he heard:"Little Qiu, you just wait me at the door, don't go away!"

BrilliantTalent Wang went forward to the safe box, stretched his fingers with a feeling as if they were shocked electrically, picked another small thing—a same doll looked like the former one—at the same time, noticed the things in his safe box were turned over.

In one drawer for bonds and shares, twenty one bonds with a denomination of one thousand with annual rate of 7.2% were missing, there were an extra pile of cash in the place with a denomination of ten dollars to one cent, the total number was seven hundred eighty one dollars sixteen cents.

In one drawer of the safe box, in first place there was a pile of cash, similar thing happened to them. There were ten pile of crispy notes, each pile had ten notes, one note was one hundred dollar, the total amount was ten thousands. The original thick pile became a thin one. Only five one hundred dollar bills were left. Strange! There were four ten dollar notes and one five dollar note, thus the total amount was five hundred forty five dollars now from ten thousands dollars.

My goodness! My safe box was stolen! The thief was really courteous! He stole two bundles of huge amount, and left some changes to him. It was unheard before that a thief would leave some changes behind! But what did that mean?

He fell into a blank status, as if he were in night-walking.

While he was stupefied, he smelled the stinky bloody burning cloth again, the smell was floating into his nostrils from time to time. At the same time, he suddenly noticed there were faint bloodstains on the extra bills left behind in his safe box. He at once realized that ten thousands minus five hundred forty five was equal to nine thousand four hundred fifty five dollars! My goodness, that was the amount he picked up from the under bed with money immersed by blood! Based on same thinking, the bonds were taken away with same meaning. Maybe the money was used to cover the silver coins, gold jewelries and other ornaments. It might be much better for him not thinking in the direction, as soon as he thought about the thing, it seemed that his soul had been driven into a horrible and mad hole!

Nevertheless, his mind still could keep its calmness. Though he was in a confused status, he still did not lose his common sense completely. He thought further and carefully, sensed something was wrong for what he was facing: Do a ghost have an ability to drive a paper doll to move something out of the safe box? The story he developed twelve years ago was used to deceive people, how could paper dolls become alive in such fashion? If the thing happens without any involvement of a ghost, then someone might try to make something out of the thing secretly. Then who is behind the thing? He thinks only one person could access the key of the safe box, the person is his wife PendantJade. Did she steal the money and bonds in the safe box? Nevertheless, she is a frugal person, why she needs that large amount of money? Even if she needs the money for some emergency, she could talk to him openly and directly, is it necessary to steal the money by her? Even if she stole the money and the bonds, why she would use the horrible paper doll as a trick? Furthermore, the stealing is implicated with the paper dolls. If the incident is done by someone, the person must be very good at calculation with a careful thinking and design. As to Pendantjade, she did not know much words with a simple mind. Thus, she did not have a reason to play such a kind of trick and that kind of intelligence to do such a kind of trick. Furthermore, someone is definitely behind the trick, the reason is that he did not mention the thing happened twelve years ago to anyone else including her. Who could know the story of paper dolls? Who could know the exact amount in the thing so clearly?

The most important thing is that he saw the man who was executed twelve years ago twice, which is impossible for someone to act. Just based on the fact, it must be the ghost who stole the money.

If the thing was done by the ghost, he took away nine thousand four hundred and fifty dollars in cash and a pile of bonds to compensate the silver coins and gold jewelries. If he shows up again, he definitely will come to claim his life to avenge his own death!

The more he thought about the thing, the more afraid he became.

In the day, when he rushed out of the room with his apprehensive and horrible expression, the expression transfixed Little Qiu who was waiting outside of the room.

Horrible thing came one after another. There were two more incidents of blood stained paper doll: One time the doll was found in a book on his desk; another time the doll was found in the pocket of his shirt. Furthermore, every time around the doll was found, there was a bloody smell of burning cloth. In the day with the strongest smell, he came across the ghost again!

That time was in an early misty morning, they came across in the glass building within his garden, at that time he was inside the building, and the ghost was standing at the outside of the building, he looked at the condemned one who was executed by being cut out his heart through the glass!

The ghost changed his clothes due to season, did not wear the same clothes they came across each other last time. His clothes changed back to the clothes he had worn twelve years ago when he first came to the hostel Spring Flower in the night: A worn-out thick pelt hat on his head and a dirty black cotton padded jacket with a big hole on his shoulder of the jacket. The looking of the hat and the clothes were kept in his memory, with just a reminder, the memory flashed into his mind clearly and rapidly, there was a still blue apron around his waist just like twelve years before, though he could not see his shoes, they must be the straw sandals covered with mud. He held a small cloth package, though it was not a rainy day, he still held a broken oil umbrella.

In a word, he looked exactly like a copy from the same press plate of twelve years ago!

At the moment, the ghost grinned which exposed his brown teeth, gave him a sad and horrible smile after they saw each other again! Later, he thought for all his life that was the most horrible experience he had ever had.

At the moment as he was terrified by what he was looking, he stared at the ghost with his widely opened eyes for quite a long time. Therefore, he noticed his feature more clearly and vividly. He clearly noticed the horrible steel-fork-like wrinkles, the black moles with several hairs on the left ear. Yes, he noticed everything, if he were not the NinthOne Tao whose heart was cut out in the year, then whom else could he be?

My goodness! Ghost! Ghost! Ghost! A ghost in daytime! Could he doubt about that anyway?

Chapter 8 Well, Let Me Confess, I Must Confess!

From then on, there was an abnormal and spooky air enshrouding the house of BrilliantTalent Wang—all servants of the house got the same air from his horrible expression! But they did not understand why their host had that kind of horrible expression?

Since he met the ghost for third time, in the night, he thought his body temperature was not right; when he saw himself in a mirror, he noticed he lost his former looking as he became much thinner. But he was a well-known man, thus he had to keep his good image as possibly as he could in day. He was afraid that the thing he did in twelve years ago was found by other people, thus though he felt bad about his body, he still tried his best to move on and did not want to admit that he had a illness. Even he had a merciful wish to ask some monks to pray for the condemned one, thus the ghost could enter the heaven above to become an immortal. But due to his misgiving for the same reason, he hesitated about the thing, in the end the pray was not done as he wished.

Thus, the well-known man probably had already gotten to experience what he deserved.

Of course for the time being, he had been receiving medical care continuously. The doctor he visited most frequently was a doctor with a medical degree, he was over sixty years old and well-known in society. His name was ForPeople Xia.

Dr. Xia knew the cause of his illness, the illness was a depression caused by some stimulus, but he just could not find the cause for his depression. He could only persuade BrilliantTalent Wang to have more recreational activities to ease the tension of his nerves.

He accepted the advice gladly, but to where to have his recreational activities? Movie, he did not want to see another film at all; ballroom, he did not have any interest for dance. In the end, he accepted the suggestion of Little Qiu: he went to a tea house to while away his time.

They spent several mornings in Big East tea house. He felt he had relaxed quite a bit in his spirit. For recent period, what he needed most was bustling place with a lot of people; he was afraid of a quiet and empty place. Thus the place had given a lot of consoles he wanted for the time being. Unexpectedly, in the day another incident happened which was beyond anyone's imagination again.

As to the mysterious incident happened twelve years ago, the incident happened in the tea house could be taken as a magical stick, due to the stick, the screen of the mysterious and winding incident was uncovered to some extent. If the incident did not happen in the day, whether the mysterious incident happened twelve years ago which was beyond the imagination of ordinary people with their normal intelligence would be solved and known to people in such a short time, none could be sure about that.

The thing happened as following:

In the day he had a good spirit, he was having a good conversation with Little Qiu. In a seat next them a man was smoking a kind of cigarette imported from Turkey. Strong smokes were floating to them from time to time. For recent days he was in an extremely worrying status, the hysteria was hiding in his body to wait its chance to pop out as the hysteria had been strengthened for quite a while, particularly he had already developed a psychological status, thus he would be easily stimulated by anything as he even suspected a little snake was hiding in his little tea cup. At the moment, maybe due to the strong smoke of the cigarette, for unknown reason, he suddenly had an illusion: He mistook the smoke as the stinky smell of the burning cloth, thus while he was talking in sitting position, suddenly, he stared his eyes widely open, could not help but shout:"My goodness! It showed up again! The ghost with a mole on his ear!"

The neurotic shouting drew all the attentions of the people in the house on him as if they were all shooting at him with their gazes. Particularly there was a man near them, upon hearing the shouting, he immediately turned his head to look at him. There was an extremely surprising expression on the face of the man—maybe the expression could be described as a panic one.

The man was the one who was smoking the cigarette. The man wore a dark green suit with thin sliver stripes and a violet necktie. He had a haircut of Philippine style with his pointed shiny black leather shoes. On first appearance, he was quite young.

At the moment, the man who was smoking the cigarette noticed BrilliantTalent Wang left the house hurriedly with support of Little Qiu under the gaze of the people. The man called the waiter, settled his account, took his overcoat and hat in his hand, hurriedly followed them and came out of the room.

At the roadside, he took out his notebook, jotted down the plate number of the new style car.

In next morning around nine o'clock, at the entrance of a French style villa—that was the house of BrilliantTalent Wang—came two people with suits one after another. The front one was taking a black leather bag which was quite worn out, he was Dr. Xia. The latter was also taking a black leather bag with an exquisite stethoscope in one hand. In such fashion, he was telling people that he was a doctor without any doubt.

When Dr. Xia stepped on the smooth step stone, the latter walked a bit fast, came to shoulder to shoulder with Dr. Xia, said as if they had known each other quite well:"Dr. Xia, good morning!"

Before Dr. Xia saw the man's face, he first noticed the leather bag and the stethoscope, thought to himself:"The illness of BrilliantTalent Wang must have changed to some extent. Otherwise, how he would ask another doctor?"

Before Dr. Xia could open his mouth to reply, the man introduced himself:" I am Dr. ShadowChange Yu. My clinic is located nearby."

"I've heard so much about you!" When Dr. Xia said the words, actually he did not know the man at all just like his strange name.

They walked shoulder to shoulder to the gate of the house, the people of the house thought they worked together and the young man was an assistant of Dr. Xia.

In the day BrilliantTalent Wang could not persist any longer, he had to stay in bed. In his luxurious room which was decorated as a royal one, besides the patient, there were two other people. One was a young woman about twenty six to seven years old with a disheveled black hairs. She wore a cheongsam of blue cloth. She wore a haggard expression with a faint powder on her face, which made her look delicate and touching—at the corners of her eyes, there was a worried expression. It seemed that she was bothered by some unhappy thing in her heart—the young woman with plain clothes was his wife, PendantJade. The other one was a sturdy youth, he wore a gray flannel gown, he was Little Qiu.

When the old and the young doctors entered the room, the patient was staring at the roof, he was murmuring something in a very low voice. His voice was low and weak, people in the room did not hear what he was talking about—or maybe they did not pay attention what he was talking about? Only ShadowChange Yu who followed Dr. Xia paid high attention to the talking patient, it seemed his hearing was quite good. Thus he immediately understood that the patient was murmuring:"Well, let me confess, I must confess!"

In fact the patient did not lose his mind and was not in a confused status. When he saw the old doctor, he immediately nodded his head slightly on his pillow, then said in a low voice:"Dr. Xia, morning." While talking, he was watching the strange man behind Dr. Xia with a bit surprised expression just like PendantJade and Little Qiu.

"Well! Mr. Wang, how about your feeling today?" The old doctor always started his visit with same words.

Then Dr. Xia began to do his routine check: Take temperature, count pulse, listen to heart. Dr. Yu just offered his help as needed at the side. When he noticed Dr. Xia taking a syringe out of his bag, he immediately lighted the alcohol burner to sterilize the syringe first. His action was quick and appropriate, his attitude was extremely earnest.

Yes, he was doing something for someone else, but he did not suffer a bit loss in the process. At the moment, the young assistant who was not invited to come to the room left a good impression to Dr. Xia. Dr. Xia thought he was not just a novice in the field, with his earnest and kind attitude, he had the virtue to be a good doctor in future, which was quite rare!

Thus, they began to chat about the case of the patient.

"His heart is very weak, he could not have a good sleep every night, it is really a bad thing!" While focusing his attention on the syringe in his hand to expel the air out of the syringe, the old doctor said:" Furthermore, he has a gastric problem. In order to treat his gastric illness, I have tried to add several percent of the extract solution of nux vomica in my own medicine mixture. You know the solution is extracted from nux vomica. If it is used properly, it could be used to treat gastric illness, nevertheless—"

The old doctor just frowned a bit, did not continue his words.

"Yes! The reaction to the extract is annoying. Therefore, we have to be careful when we decide the amount of the extract." Dr. Yu looked at the knit eyebrows of Dr. Xia, echoed his words immediately. Based on his tone, he was so sure and experienced. As a matter of fact, that was the first time he heard about the nux vomica since he had his own ears.

After he finished his check and treatment, left his prescription, Dr. Xia left in haste. But Dr. Yu still stayed in the place, he did not have any intention to leave the place. Dr. Xia thought he was a doctor invited by the family. Of course Dr. Yu had to do his own check and diagnosis, thus he did not say anything else, just left.

After Dr. Xia left, Dr. Yu told the wife of the patient:" Dr. Xia left two pills to the patient. He enjoined: I have to observe the patient for two to three hours to determine whether it is necessary to give the pills to the patient. Thus, I will stay in this place for several hours."

When he was waiting for the period of time, Dr. Yu who looked very young walked around the house as he were walking around his own house without any reservation.

He walked to the front of the garage, had a chat with the driver Old Li for a while. Then he chatted with the personal guard, WideSouth Cao, from BaoDing City and acknowledged that they were from same city, thus they should be taken as fellow-townsmen. Then he chatted with the gardener ThirdVaue Zhang for several sentences. He then chatted with chef, little maidservant etc. for a while. His communication skill was so excellent—as if his skill were with some magic power—based on his talk, he would know the personality and psychology of the talked, and would talk accordingly. His words were interesting and funny, he would make everyone laugh when he talked with them. In less than two hours, everyone in the house thought he was more affable and kind than the staid old doctor.

In the noon, the house offered him an exquisite free lunch. After the lunch, it seemed that he had to do something, thus he took two pills of soda which was very cheap from his bag, gave the pills to the wife in a serious tone, let the patient swallow the pills, which should be taken as his payback for the free lunch. Then he lighted a cigarette imported from Turkey, breathed several rings of smoke, wiped his mouth, and left the house.

Chapter 9 You Were Quite Good At Sketching!

In next morning, around eight o'clock, Dr. Xia got a call, was told the call from Wang's house and the patient felt quite good, wanted to go to park, thus his visit should be suspended for one day.

But around the same time of previous day—nine o'clock—Dr. ShadowChange Yu came alone with his bag and entered the house and went into the room of the patient as if he visited the house frequently.

At the moment, besides the patient, his wife PendantJade and a maidservant, the earnest Little Qiu had already arrived in the room too. Little Qiu worked as the chief accountant in ConstructChina Company which was famous in Shanghai. For last several days, due to his master's illness, he took several days off to take care of his master. At the moment he was preparing a cup of fresh milk with a silver spoon to mix a sugar cube, then he touched the spoon at the tip of his tongue to check the temperature of the milk. The carefulness proved their deep relationship as master and student.

The youth raised his head, saw Dr. Yu entering the room, hurriedly put down the cup in his hand, said:"Good morning, Dr. Yu!"

The wife looked at him questioningly as if she had wanted to ask:"Why Dr. Xia does not come here?"

Dr. Yu said loudly:"Dr. Xia has two emergencies today, he could not arrange his time, thus he let me come here first."

Upon finishing his words, he began to check the patient as if he were acting for a show. When he was doing his check, he heard the patient was still murmuring like yesterday from time to time.

While Dr. Yu was writing his illegible prescription, he suddenly said to the wife:" I am sorry, Mrs. Wang, could you stay in another room for a while, I want to do some thorough investigation for the patient."

The words of the doctor were equal to an order, though the woman was surprised about the demand, but she did not say anything. The young man gave the cup of the milk to the patient, without saying any word, left the room with the maidservant.

PendantJade and Little Qiu stayed in a resting room across the room for quite a while patiently. What's wrong? Why the thorough investigation had not finished yet. They walked to the room several times, pushed the door, but it was locked from inside, the room was very quiet, nothing could be heard in the room, they just could not understand what was going on in the room.

They waited for more than ninety minutes, they heard a light knocking sound, at the same time the door of the resting room opened lightly and quickly, the young doctor showed up at the door. At the moment, the young man and woman were talking in a low voice at a corner of the room. When the door opened, the shadow in front of the window was divided into two parts, they raised their heads simultaneously, noticed Dr. Yu held a cigarette in one hand while another hand was in his pocket, walked into the room leisurely while whistling. He wore a happy expression on his face.

"Well! Mrs. Wang, I have to report to you—" he said in a joyful tone," I think Mr. Wang's illness will be cured very soon."

"Thank you, Dr. Yu, that's all your and Dr. Xia's credit. We have to express our greatest gratitude to you both," The young woman said gratefully. There was a specific worried expression on her face.

"Dr. Yu, do you think, Mr. Wang has some kind of nerve disease?" the tall young man Little Qiu interrupted.

"It seems like that." Dr. Yu looked at the young man with neat clothes, said:"Based on my observation, his illness is due to inconsolable depression. Do you know any specific cause about his depression?"

"You are right. Dr. Xia asked him a long time ago, less alone us, he just did not want to say anything specific to anyone," she said with a frown.

" I heard recently Mr. Wang becomes a bit nervous, right?" Dr. Yu exhaled a smoke, while one heel of his shoe wheeled on the carpet from left to right.

"This—" Her thin eyebrows frowned a bit again. She just uttered the word, then Little Qiu interrupted, said:" In recent months, my master has done some deals involved in gold, the amount involved is huge, there is a huge swing in price, which is frightening! Maybe his illness is related to the business." It seemed he used the words either to answer for her or to explain to the doctor.

Dr. Yu nodded his head to express his acceptance about the explanation, said:"After his recovery, you have to persuade him to spend some time to take care of flowers and golden fish, or to learn draw some paintings, which is very good for his health." While they were talking to here, it seemed that Dr. Yu recalled something related to drawing, asked unintentionally to the young man:" Well,

Mr. Qiu, I came across you once in Academy of Fine Arts. Did you study in the school before?"

"No! You might have made a mistake for someone else." Little Qiu looked at the doctor.

"But you have painted very good about still life."

"Just for fun. I occasionally paint once or twice, how could they be taken as paintings." Little Qiu said modestly and unintentionally, but there was a bit gladness in his tone.

"But you are quite good at sketching human figure," Dr. Yu said suddenly with a bit raised voice.

"Uh, Ahem!" At the moment, the young woman made a light coughing sound, which was inserted into their conversation.

"Sketching about human figure?!" Little Qiu cast a glance quickly at PendantJade, noticed there was a weird expression in the eyes of the doctor, immediately realized something, hesitated a bit, said in a very serious tone:" Human sketch! I could not do that, I could only do traditional Chinese painting, that is the still life painting in Chinese style."

"Really! Like banana, apple etc., right?" A string of round circles of smoke came out of the mouth of the doctor, the halos of the smokes could not cover up a bit smile at the corners of his mouth which barely noticeable.

They fell into a short silence. The room was filled with quietness, there was a bit of tense atmosphere within the quietness.

"Let me go to his room to have a look, there is none in his room," she said in a gentle voice to break the silence.

"Mrs. Wang, you need not to worry about him!" The doctor went to the door at once, blocked the door, said:"I know Mr. Wang is afraid of quietness, thus I have already called a lot of people going into the room to accompany him. The driver, the gardener, the concubine from HuZhou and the maidservant all are in the room, the room is filled with people, thus you needn't to worry about that."

While saying, Dr. Yu took out a piece of paper from his pocket—on the back of the paper, he jotted down a lot of Arabic numerals, it seemed that the numbers constituted a complex multiple formula. On the front of the paper, he wrote down a clear sentence—he handed the paper to her, said:" This is his medical bill, please check the number, whether it is right or not?"

She took the paper into her hand, just with a glance, she showed a puzzled expression, shouted surprisingly:"My goodness! What kind of drugs? How could it be so expensive?"

The shouting drew Little Qiu forward, he noticed there was a line written by a fountain pen on the paper:

Total cost for medicine: Nine Thousand Four Hundred And Fifty Dollars.

The mysterious figure made the color of the face of the young man change at once! He was transfixed for more than ten seconds, then asked surprisingly:"Dr. Yu, what do you mean?"

"I mean: There are two or more than two people acting together to prepare a medicine, thus they have already collected nine thousand four hundred fifty five dollars as a fee to manufacture the medicine." He took the paper back from the hand of the young woman, shrugged once while saying the words.

"I don't understand!" Little Qiu said loudly.

The cheeks of the young woman turned pale at once, she could only appreciate at the flower patterns in the carpet silently.

"Don't you both understand? It's okay if you don't understand. I have a complicated story to tell you. I got to know the story in less than an hour ago." Dr. Yu waved his hand to them as if a host were greeting his guests, said:"How about you both sit down, just listen my words quietly. Upon hearing my words, you both will understand it completely."

Chapter 10 I Persuaded Him To Tell The Thing Buried Deep Into His Heart To Me Completely

At the moment, the three people in the room wore various interesting expressions:

The young woman raised her hesitating eyes, it seemed that she was a bit flustered. She looked at Little Qiu blankly as if she wanted to follow his decision. Little Qiu was a bit frightened by the sharp gaze of the doctor as he knew nothing about this weird guy, who was the guy? Why he talked those strange words? What did he want?—He was filled with questions and doubts. As result, in such a short and flustered moment, he took a seat in a sofa at the dim corner of the room near the hanging curtain. The woman took another seat which was some distance away from the one Little Qiu occupied in a confused fashion as she noticed Little Qiu took a seat. She took out a handkerchief from her pocket, began to fiddle with it subconsciously and continuously.

They both looked at the mysterious doctor, the doctor flipped the stub of his cigarette away into a spittoon at the corner of the room several yards from him, turned and closed the door, then pulled his trousers a bit, sat in a cushioned chair near the door with a leisure and comfortable position.

The three people in the room sat in a triangular fashion though the sides were not equal.

Dr. Yu was a heavy smoker, could not have his mouth rest for a long time, thus lighted another cigarette for himself. In the silent atmosphere for the time being, it seemed that he began to show off his skill of breathing circles of smoke. He crossed his one leg on another, shook the shiny leather shoe cap, exhaled the smoke for quite a while, then began to talk about his story.

"For two days from yesterday, I heard Mr. Wang murmured that he wanted to make a confession. I know there must be some interesting story behind his words. Thus, I did make a special opportunity to talk with him alone, prepared to use hook made of my tongue to get out of his secret buried in his heart."

Among the heavy halos of smoke of the imported cigarette from Turkey, the young man and the young woman were listening quietly, uneasily and attentively about his story.

"I told him I am a reliable Christian, he should take me as a priest, tell me what he dared not to tell anyone about the thing buried deep into his heart, which should be taken as an earnest confession."

The young man and the young showed an anxious expression, as if they were asking:"Then, in the end, did he tell you or not?"

"At the beginning, Mr. Wang did not want to tell me, he persisted that he would only confess to a monk of Buddhism. Therefore I tried a method of threatening and inveigling to make him confess:

"The thing happened in a mysterious fashion. Mr. Wang said: Twelve years ago, he worked at a hotel as a manager in a town of ZheJiang Province. In one night, there was a man coming to the hotel, he found the man was a remnant member of White Lotus Society, could cut paper dolls from a piece of white paper, let the dolls go around to take out the livers and hearts of children. At that time, in order to get rid of the evil man who could bring damage to the local people, he went to a local powerful man, got the man arrested. On the spot, they found several paper dolls in the package of the man with birth dates of several children in red paper slips—"

When the doctor talked to thus far, he noticed a sad and melancholy shadow flashing across the face of the woman, then a despising expression on her face as she curled her lips slightly. He could not understand the reaction of the woman for the time being, thus he just continued:

"At the moment, they decided to cut out the heart and liver of the man alive based on some kind of barbarian law, which was extremely cruel! It was said they did that for avenging those victims of children. At the same time, it was funny they attached the paper dolls found from the package to the chest of the man, it was said they wanted to execute the dolls with the man together—"

When he talked to here, he noticed there was a circle of reddish color in the eyes of the woman. She took a chance of winking her eyes, turned her face aside, wiped the corners of her eyes with her handkerchief in her hand.

The young woman thought her little action was not noticed by the doctor, and the doctor pretended he had not noticed her little action, he continued:

"Before the man was executed, he made a swear, he said: Though I will die, my vengeful ghost will climb out of my grave in daytime, I will find my enemy and claim his life!"

The doctor paused, within the smokes of his cigarette, he saw they kept their silence. As it was a horrible story, it seemed that the air of the room turned a bit weird.

The doctor continued:"The sorcerer left a package with gold jewelry, silver coins, other jewelry and bank notes, the total amount was nine thousand four hundred fifty five dollars. Well, Mrs. Wang and Mr. Qiu, please pay your attention to the number! Now, I will go to my point—"

The doctor paused suddenly, scanned their faces with his cold gaze alternately, then continued in a calm tone:

"After the sorcerer died, the package belonged to none. Thus, Mr. Wang took the package by himself in secret fashion without any courtesy. The thing happened twelve years ago, none knew anything about that. Unexpectedly, something weird happened in recent days—recently, Mr. Wang who wanted to get rid of sorcerer for the people while upholding justice came across the executed man inside and outside of his house who died twelve years ago, at the same time he found the horrible paper dolls covered with blood! The above thing is the cause of his illness due to fright and depression and worry, what he wanted to confess is also the thing—"

"Well! You need not to be haste, there were still some weird things."

"Several days ago, Mr. Wang found the blood stained paper doll had already crawled into his safe box, furthermore, the money and bonds he kept in the box were missing. He lost twenty one bonds with a denomination of one thousand, the total amount was twenty one thousands. The thing was not a bit strange, what strange was that the thief politely left some paper money with changes, just like a shop owner gave some changes to his customer when the customer gave him a banknote with high denomination. Well, let me see, what was the total amount of the change?"

He took out the slip from his pocket, read it again, then continued:"The change was seven hundred eight one dollars sixteen cents. It is really weird. How could the thief steal in such unique fashion with so strange an amount, what does that mean?"

The doctor paused his speaking, he cast a questioning gaze at them, it seemed that he was waiting for their answer, but they kept their silence, thus he could only answer the question by himself:"Let's just forget about the thing related to bonds for a moment, let's talk about the money lost. Among the cash of ten thousand dollars, thief took all the money except he left five hundred forty five dollars. That is ten thousand minus five hundred forty five? The number is what I have already told you before, and you both should know the number."

He took another smoke, before they could answer, he continued:"Based on the opinion of Mr. Wang, he thought the steal was related to the ghost, the ghost sent the paper dolls to take the money away. He recalled the past incident, was scared to death, but the steal was related to the past incident, thus he dared not to speak out."

"Above story was told me by Mr. Wang. The story is really weird. But there are somethings in the story which need one to think further." The doctor squinted his eyes, said in a witty tone:"You just think about it, why the ghost did not go to the tinfoil shop to steal tinfoil(* Which is still used to make silver coins to use in another world for the dead till moment), why the ghost comes to a house to steal the bonds and cash, isn't it funny? If the thing was done by a ghost, we are not famous Master Zhang or Master Wang of Taoist to catch the ghost, which is beyond our power. Nevertheless, we just make a supposition: The thing was done by a human, then we should think who is the person acting like a ghost?"

"Mr. Wang thought about the possibility, there was a suspecting cloud fleeting across his mind once. He thought: only one person has the possibility to get the key. The person is—"

He paused at the moment, cast a cold gaze at her face.

"Whom?" The woman asked loudly with a crimson face.

"It's you!" The doctor said in a cold voice to finish the sentence.

"It's me! It's me! That is just a bullshit from a biting dog! Those are words from his dream! He is a man who is wrong with his head, do you have—same kind illness like him!?" The young woman stood up angrily from her chair, lost completely the demure and gentle manner she kept a moment ago.

Chapter 11 Who Are You? What Kind of Right Do You Have To Interfere The Family Matter?

At the moment, the jugulars of Little Qiu who sat at the dim corner silently became distended obviously. It seemed that he could not take it anymore, he opened his mouth, it seemed that he wanted to say something, in the end, he did not utter a sound.

The doctor said coldly and calmly:"Well, Mrs. Wang, please calm down, you just let me finish my words. I am only talking about a supposition." He looked at the woman with crimson face with an oppressing expression, it seemed that he wanted to send her a warning signal:"Hi! You know what you did, it is much better for you to sit down."

It seemed that the woman could not endure the oppressing gaze, as if she had wanted to throw something away, she plopped down into the sofa again.

"Well, Mrs. Wang, let's suppose: You opened the safe box. But—" The doctor still looked at the woman with the oppressing expression, continued:" you cannot finish that kind of thing by yourself. At least you should have one accomplice to plan and implement. As to the accomplice, it is needless to say he must have close relationship with a person in this room."

Little Qiu's breath became shallow and rapid, his breathing sound could be heard during the pause of the the talk. At the moment his dry lips twitched once.

The doctor did not wait the young man to say anything, continued:" Thus, I remembered the mysterious paper dolls mentioned by Mr. Wang—when Mr. Wang received those unique gifts, he particularly kept one for himself. At the moment, he pointed the hiding place to me, let me take the doll to have a look."

Little Qiu stared his eyes widely open, heard he said in an sarcastically praising voice as if he were exclaiming something marvellous:

"Well, look, isn't this little thing marvellous! You just look at the lines, the charm strokes, the vivid cuttings. If one just has one look, one definitely is sure the thing must come from someone who is very good at painting. Maybe, this doll is the master piece of the accomplice. Of course we cannot be sure this thing must come from the accomplice, but if one thinks from various angles, it is highly possible this thing is from the accomplice."

At the moment, the doctor did not show anymore courtesy to the young man, began to take an offensive action against him, said:" Mr. Qiu, I think you are highly possible to be the accomplice. Thus, I asked around do you know painting before? Thank you very much, you just told me bluntly: You really do know the drawing skill."

The young man could not hold it off any longer, clenched his fist, pounded down at the armrest of the sofa with a force, jumped up as if he were a released spring from the sofa, said angrily and loudly:" I have already told you that 'I don't draw a portrait.' Are you deaf?"

Then he added:"You just ask around, do anyone know I draw a portrait?"

"You are absolutely right. As nobody knows you are able to draw a portrait, thus you could do it without a bit scruple!" the doctor still kept his calm expression, said in a cold tone. " Furthermore, when I was asking the question, I had already prepared that you would tell me that you don't know how to draw a portrait."

The young man wore a livid expression, his breath became even more rapid, his words were choked at his throat.

The doctor continued:" Whether you could draw a portrait or not, it is just a little matter, Isn't it? Mr. Qiu, if there were nothing wrong, how could you speak in that kind of angry tone, why did you pay a high attention to the question?"

"You couldn't just crush someone to death only by your words!" The young man mustered all his courage, mumbled.

"Well, do you want to blackmail us?" PendantJade who wore angry expression suddenly blurted out the words for no reason.

The doctor chose to ignore their words, while smoking, he continued calmly:" Well, I still have some other evidences. I just said: To be an accomplice, the person has to satisfy several conditions: first, the person has to have an intimate relationship with this house; second, the person has to know how to draw a portrait. In addition, the person—"

The doctor took out the slip again from his pocket, while holding the slip in his hand, he said:" Mr. Wang told me besides the bonds with 7.2% interest rate, there were shares and other bonds. The thief did not take the shares and other bonds, but the bonds with 7.2% interest rate, because the bonds are well-received in market and they could be sold easily. Thus, you know the person must know the bond market very well. What do you think, could it take as another clue?"

He paused for a moment, then continued:" If the thing could be taken as an evidence, it is not very strong, but there is still more." He read the slip in his hand once, said:"I have already told you that the total amount of the bonds lost is twenty-one thousands, but the thief left seven hundred eighty one dollar and sixteen cents behind. Thus the exact amount of the loss should be twenty thousands two hundred eighteen dollars eighty-four cents. The thief took that kind of amount, just like he took away the cash of nine thousand four hundred fifty-five dollars, he definitely wanted to signify something meaningful. Mr. Wang was frightened shit out of him at the moment. He could not figure out the reasons behind the acts. Based on my coarse calculation, the strange number is from the exact number of nine thousand four hundred fifty-five dollars, that means the number is the interest for twelve years. Based on ten percent annual rate, the number is based on compound interest for twelve years. Thus, we get another clue, the Mr. Accomplice is a talent who knows how to calculate compound interest."

When the doctor spoke thus far, he sat up from a reclining position, shrugged to the young man once, said with a grimace:" Well, let me summarize the conditions to be an accomplice! First, he must have close relationship with this house; second, he knows to draw a portrait; third, he knows bond market; fourth, he knows how to calculate a compound interest. My goodness, aren't the conditions too many!"

He blinked his eyes once, said in a slow and low voice:" But you, Mr. Qiu, satisfy all the conditions I mentioned above. If it is a coincidence, then it is too coincidental! Well, Mr. Qiu, do you want to say anything about my analysis?"

The doctor finished his words, folded the flip and put it back into his pocket again, took out another cigarette from the pack, knocked the cigarette gently on the exquisite pack for a while, took out his elegant lighter, tried to light his cigarette. His manner was easy and calm, in contrast Little Qiu was with nervous expression, did not utter a sound for the time being with his reddish face. Based on his despondent attitude, it seemed that he acknowledged his total failure, and there was no chance for him to bounce back.

The woman who was in same defense line with the young man noticed her ally was attacked violently, looked at the man with a pitiful expression, at the same time she wore an embarrassed expression.

After he hesitated for several seconds, it seemed that the young man mustered enough courage, he wanted to attack the doctor from another line, said:"Who are you? Do you have any right to interfere things happening in this house!?"

"As a doctor, he notices his patient is about to send a crematorium or an asylum, does not he have a right to interfere?" the doctor asked in reply in a leisure fashion.

"You are merely a doctor, you are not an official, you don't have any right to interfere our things." She began to make her counterattack based on the words of Little Qiu and at the same time she had already mustered enough courage.

The doctor ignored her words, just talked to him, said:" Haven't you asked who am I? I have to tell you who I am. Do you still remember two days ago when you accompanied your teacher to go to the tea house. He shouted for no reason:'My goodness, he showed up again, the evil ghost with a mole on his ear!' At the moment, his nervous shouting surprised me."

The rigid man and woman did not understand his meaning, they could only stare at him and wait for his further explanation.

"At that time, why I was surprised?" The doctor said:"It's a shame to me! Unfortunately, for my life, I am often mistaken as an evil ghost, furthermore, it happens I have a mole on my ear. Therefore, at the moment I thought your master had already recognized my face mask—you know, my mask, like the one of the many so-called great men in the world, should not be exposed by any other people, that is the reason why I was surprised. At the same time, which made me to take part in your great play, do you understand?" While talking, he stretched his slightly bent body forward, turned his head a bit, pointed his left ear with his hand, let the young man watch his ear.

Little Qiu staggered forward for several steps, noticed the mole on his left ear, about size of a green pea as red as a little star.

What a strange mole! The tiny red spot had a magical power which was equal to a new comet found by an astronomer with a telescope; at the same time, the tiny spot was reflected on his pupils, it seemed that he was as scary as BrilliantTalent Wang when he had noticed the mole on the ear of the ghost in the day!

The young man stared his eyes widely open due to fright, a frightened word was sent to the tip of his tongue, said:"You!"

"Sh, sh!" The doctor hurriedly put two fingers on his lips to cover his mouth and assumed a frightened and mysterious manner, said:"Well! It means nothing once you know the answer, anyway, as you have already noticed the honest label of mine, probably you already have gotten what kind of person I am. Therefore, the most smart way is you tell me the truth."

He waved his hand gently to them, meant they should take their seats. The young man surveyed his face for a while, then could not do anything but to return his seat near the side of the window. The woman, though she did not know why Little Qiu became frightened in that weird fashion, felt bewildered, took her seat for third time.

Chapter 12 How About Let Me Explain, Okay?

When the doctor saw they both sat down again, he returned his slack and calm status. He yawned first, then looked at their faces alternately, said in a lazy voice:" Problems have to be solved one by one. First, please tell me: Who took the bonds and cash away from the safe box?"

His gaze first stopped at the face of Little Qiu.

" "
...

"Speak out, now!"

Little Qiu raised his head, then immediately lowered his head again, at the moment it seemed a stage light was focusing on his face: his reddish face turned a bit white, then a bit bluish color, in the end completely gray.

The woman cast Little Qiu a secret glance, noticed his embarrassing expression, hesitated a bit, suddenly mustered up her courage, said loudly:" I took the money!"

"Good!" The doctor nodded his head, said in a slow and low voice intentionally:" It is quite common for a wife to take the money from her husband."

"No! I took the money!" At last Little Qiu was forced to open his mouth.

"Good!" The doctor nodded his head, said: " As a student, in case he had an emergency , it could not be taken as a theft if he took some money from his master for a short while."

"Not him, but me."

"Not her, but me."

Due to an emotional impulse, it seemed that they both forgot the embarrassing situation they were in at the moment, they became so generous and wanted to shoulder the responsibility by oneself only.

"Well, well! I think your feeling to each other just like a French style hot coffee!" The doctor flicked the little ash on his cigarette, said while smiling.

A faint red color flied to her cheeks which were still holding some reddish color due to anger.

Upon hearing the words, Little Qiu became angry again, but when he noticed the tiny red spot on his ear, he could only humph lightly once to let out of his anger.

"Then why did you want to take the bonds and cash?" The doctor looked at Little Qiu while asking.

"Of course, for an emergency," Little Qiu forced himself to calm down, hesitated for a moment, then said. He cast a glance once at the door which was not closed tightly, said in a low and begging voice:" If—if you are willing to keep the secret for me, I will tell you the truth."

"You should remember," the doctor pointed at his mole again, " the man with a red mole on his ear is the most kind, honest, and upright person who is willing to keep a secret for anyone, you just feel assured."

"Well! Then, I will tell you the truth—" he said in a voice full of emotions, " Really, I took the bonds and cash as recently I bought some gold bullion, I lost quite a lot, I could not find any other solution, thus I could only do in that fashion."

"Maybe you are telling truth," the doctor nodded his head, said:" But you have to give me details."

" In fact for the bonds and cash in safe box, I took separately. First time, I only took the cash, but the money was not enough to cover the loss, thus, I took the bonds in second time." At the moment, the young man cast a glance at the woman, then said in a passionate voice:" As a man, I will take the responsibility for what I did. You should not add the theft on the head of Pendant—well, of my master's wife."

The young master's wife immediately blushed, she was about to say something, but she was stopped by the gaze of the doctor, heard the doctor said to Little Qiu:" I think: first time when you took the cash, you had already noticed the bonds with an interest of 7.2%. Therefore, when you opened the safe box for second time, you prepared the change for seven hundred eighty one dollars and sixteen cents, thus you left the change into the safe box. I mean the amount was equal to the interest for the nine thousand four hundred fifty five dollars for twelve years. Isn't it?"

Little Qiu nodded his head slightly with his crimson face without uttering a sound.

"But, there is some danger hiding in the amount! " the doctor said. " If Mr. Wang thinks about the amount carefully, based on the compound interest, he might suspect you quite easily, haven't you though about that?"

The young man lowered his head dejectedly, still kept his silence.

"Based on your explanation, then you took the money based on your emergency. Well, didn't you have any other meaning?" the doctor asked again.

"What do you mean?" Little Qiu raised his head suddenly, asked.

"If you just took the money for the money's sake, then you just took the money and bonds away, then why you left a horrible paper doll?"

"Why you ask in such foolish fashion? " It seemed that the woman forgot the situation she was in, she interrupted suddenly:" Everyone knows the disposition of BrilliantTalent, he is a stingy man, if the money in his safe box was missing for no reason, how could he not ask around and investigate? How could he act as if nothing happened?"

"You mean—" the doctor turned his gaze at the woman, said. "When he saw the horrible paper doll, he would not investigate the thing openly. Right? Based on what kind of reason you think in such fashion?"

"..." She hesitated a bit, it seemed that she regretted about her interruption a moment ago. Therefore, she could only lower her head awkwardly.

" Speak now!" the doctor urged.

"Because recently, we—" she was forced to speak. When she mentioned 'we', she immediately changed the word:" because recently I found his unmentionable thing unexpectedly—the thing he confessed to you a moment ago," she exchanged a glance with the young man, said haltingly.

"How could you know the incident? Based on his words: He did not tell anybody about the thing before, even for a word," the doctor pursued the thing.

"It does not matter for me to tell you!" As the doctor was forced her to tell, she said in a hateful voice. "In one day—" she thought for a moment, then continued:" More than ten days ago? He came back from outside, stood half a way in the staircases trembling blankly; at the moment his face looked horrible, it seemed that he had a sudden illness. In the night, he became quite drunk. In his drunken status, he told me about the horrible incident happened twelve years ago. In next morning, he forgot everything. Then later I intentionally got him drunk once, thus I got to know the details of the thing."

The doctor listened attentively while taking deep draws of his cigarette.

The woman suddenly added:" I got him drunk intentionally without any ill intention. I was really worrying about his illness, thus I only wanted to use the method to find out what's wrong with him."

The doctor nodded his head sympathetically, murmured as if he were talking to himself:"Yes, Mr. Wang told me: when he was scared and became confused half a way of the staircases, the day was his second time he came across the ghost—he still remembered that it was in Friday."

After he finished the words, the doctor closed his eyes, thought for a while, then stared his eyes widely open, said to the woman:"Well, who was the person playing as the ghost?"

"Well! What ghost? I did not know!" the woman was stupefied for a moment, then thought for a moment, in the end, she answered.

"Well! You should know," the doctor said coldly.

"What do you mean!"

"You definitely understand my words, I think."

" I—I don't know! I don't know!" The vocal cord was trembling like water waves, but she was with a steadfast expression.

The doctor could not do anything about that, turned his gaze at the young man, said:"Mr. Qiu, I think the ghost should not be acted by you, right?" Then he continued:"If one tells me that with a mask or a makeup, then one could act like someone else, he certainly is talking about something happened in a novel or a play! I definitely will not believe that kind of bullshit! Then, I still want you to tell me who is the Mr. Ghost?"

Little Qiu felt helpless, looked at her seeking her approval with a painful expression, noticed she was with a crimson face, did not give him any signal, thus said in a tone of imitating her style:" What ghost? I don't know!"

"Of course, you certainly know what I am talking about!"

"I could not understand what you are talking about completely!"

"Yes, it's right. When you were trying to draw the portrait for the Mr. Ghost, you forgot to ask his name," the doctor winked meaningfully to the young man, then said the sarcastic words.

While talking, he began to smoke his cigarette in leisure fashion, his steady face was enshrouding in his smokes, which increased his mysterious manner. At the moment, he was thinking:" Very well! The dark and mysterious veil is exposed to some extent. The mysterious paper doll has its origin now, the one who stole the money from the safe box is pinpointed. At the moment, so long as I could get to know the history of the Mr. Ghost, then the whole veil will be exposed completely." he continued his thinking:" Nevertheless, based on current situation, it still needs some my efforts to get to know the real identity of the ghost. Okay, let me ask in another direction..."

While thinking in such fashion, he opened his eyes slowly, said in a lazy voice:" Thus, you don't want to tell me who is the Mr. Ghost, right?"

At the moment, he yawned once, noticed they both lowered their heads, did not give him any response.

The situation became a stalemate, the conversation paused for the time being. Just as they were staying in the short and depressing atmosphere, suddenly they heard a voice from another direction, said in a sepulchral tone:"Then, let me tell you, okay?"

Chapter 13 You Killed My Father! You Seized His Wealth By Scheme!

The three people in the room stayed in the stalemate, at the same time they looked at the direction of sound, noticed the door was opened for about one foot, a man showed up at the door like a ghost. The man was with a not tidy black nightgown with embroidered flowers and a thick walking stick in his hand. The face of the man was horrible: His thick and dense eyebrows nearly narrowed to a line. His small eyes were emanating angry lights in the deep set eye sockets. Under the tall cheekbones, the lower part of his face formed an awl like shape which was wide in upper part and sharp in lower part.

The one was none else but the patient, BrilliantTalent Wang, who had been in an illusory status.

The patient staggered into the room, as if he had lost his balance, he could only stand by the cane in his hand. He did not speak any words first, just stared ferociously at the faces of PendantJade and Little Qiu as if he were a hungry tiger, it seemed that he wanted to gulp them down alive at any moment.

The young man and the young woman did not expect he would show up in the room, they were greatly surprised first. Then with a moment of hesitation, they understood what kind of situation they were in. At the moment, it seemed that a heavy lead was put on the back of his head, the young man lowered his head gradually bit by bit.

The face of young woman turned as red as blood, it seemed that the red might drop down in any moment. Her eyes lost their brightness, she just stared at the carpet blankly, it seemed that she was praying that the carpet could become a magic blanket, thus it would fly out of the room through the window while she was wrapped inside.

The patient stared at them for quite a while, as if he wanted to torment them with a cruel method on their nerves, thus his own nerves would be relieved for the same amount of time. He turned his body, closed the door, thought for a moment, then bolted the door from inside. Then he took his anger back for a moment, said happily to the doctor.

"Well, Dr. Yu—" he said in an excited voice, though he wore a haggard expression, his voice sounded like a healthy man. "The shadow in my heart has been cleared away by your words. You see, I'm fully cured! I really don't know how should I express my thanks to you."

"How about my suggestion?" the doctor raised his body a bit from the cushioned chair, asked in a seemingly glad voice.

"Wonderful!" The patient raised his thumb to the doctor, went to a cushioned chair near the doctor, sat down in the chair slowly. He leaned the cane on his side, said:" With your suggestion, I questioned the servants carefully: Did they see any strange person walking around the house recently without my notice? It is really a smart method!"

"What about the result?"

"I called each of them into my bedroom, questioned them carefully. I nearly questioned half of them, they just prevaricated and said they did not notice anyone! Humph! They knew the answer, but they did not want to tell me!" The patient raised his angry eyes, glanced at the face of PendantJade once, then continued in a loud voice:"Later, I questioned AutumnOrchid—a fourteen years old maidservant—she told me the truth due to my menace."

At the moment, he began to chuckle nervously in weird fashion.

"Really!" In the sharp eyes of the doctor, there was an expectant gaze.

"Based on AutumnOrchid, in last one to two months, there was a man who sneaked into the room, it seemed the man is a relative of the hostess, at the same time it seemed that the man is an opium addict, he is very poor. He often comes to borrow money, thus the hostess enjoined them to keep the secret and the thing from the host."

"Based on words of AutumnOrchid, I think in the day I came across the ghost in the staircases, the live ghost should come to my house. She said: he took a package of clothes from the kind hostess—Yes, I saw the man holding a package under his arm—" The patient said angrily:" Well, you don't want me to know! I must not be allowed knowing! Humph! Ghost play!"

"Then, who is the man?" The doctor interrupted his angry words.

"We have to ask her! We have to ask this good hostess!" The narrow and horrible eyes of the patient began to attack her face.

The breath of the woman was shallow and rapid, she did not utter a sound. She only rubbed her handkerchief in her hands subconsciously; it seemed that a hole might come out of the thin silk handkerchief through rubbing.

"Well, you don't speak, you want to feign your death! That should be fine," the patient howled. "You just don't want to be a nice person, you just want to be a ghost! Who is the live ghost? You tell me now! Now! You must tell me now!"

It seemed that the woman could not bear his abusive words anymore, she raised her head suddenly, said:" Who is he? Let me tell you, could you gulp me down due to him! He is my elder brother. He comes to visit me, is it against laws?"

Upon hearing the words, the eyes of the doctor shone once, he nodded his head lightly.

"Well, your brother!" The patient was stupefied for a moment, then said sarcastically and coldly:" Well, well, I really don't know you have that kind of decent brother! You have to forgive me for not giving him a warm reception, I am very sorry about that! Well, my good wife, amn't I a relative of your brother, why don't you introduce me to him?"

"Well, that is quite unnecessary! He is poor, you are rich, how could he be a match to you."

"Well, he is poor, I am rich, we could not be a match! Well, the words are quite reasonable. Nevertheless, as he knows we are not match, why he often shows up in front of me in daytime?"

"As an elder brother, is it illegal for him to visit his sister?"

"Yes! It is definitely not against laws for the visit. Nevertheless, you collude together to act like a ghost to frighten someone, isn't it legal too?" When the patient mentioned 'you', his angry look shot at the crouching Little Qiu like a cannon ball.

"um-hum-um-" at the moment there was a dry coughing sound which could not hold any longer like in a patient at the second stage of pulmonary tuberculosis coming out of the dim corner of the house. Little Qiu was gurgling in his throat. He wet his dry lips with his tongue from time to time as if he were a dying dog in May.

"Did I—we frighten you before?" That was her final defense. Her voice changed quite a bit, but she still persisted in her last defense line, she wanted to hold on till the end.

"You did not frighten me before! You dare to say you did not frighten me before! You, all of you, including the one who acted as a live ghost, tried to act like the dead who died twelve years ago to frighten me, do not you dare to say that you did not frighten me?" With his uncontrollable anger, the patient forgot the taboo he held for many years as a secret, while shouting, he trembled to stand up from his chair to rush toward the woman.

At the moment only calm person was the unique doctor, he was adopting lazily a half reclining position, as if he were waiting for a barber to shave his heard. It seemed to him that even the earth turned upside down, it really did not matter with him. At the moment, he sensed the fireball was about to blow up in the room, the danger had already reached to quite an extent, he could not maintain his calmness anymore. Thus, he raised his seemingly tired eyelids, said in a cold voice as if he had wanted to pour a basin of cold water down from the head of the patient:" Well, Mr. Wang, it's much better for you to calm down, you just talk with each other in quiet and calm fashion. Dr. Xia said: You should not get angry, if you get angry, you might blow up your blood vessels!"

Well, the cold water was a very effective weapon to extinguish a fire! Of course as a rich man, he was not willing to let his blood vessels blow up, thus he definitely would not take his life as cheap as one of a pig! Therefore with the words of the doctor, the patient calmed down at once. The patient immediately turned his little eyes like the ones of a mouse on the doctor, looked at him apprehensively once, immediately threw away about half of his anger.

The anger of the patient was doused down with the formless cold water at once, but when the woman heard the words 'twelve years ago', a fury flame was ignited in her elegant eyes. She stood up from her seat, clenched her teeth angrily, then laughed coldly and hatefully, said in a despising tone:"Humph! You dared to mention the thing happened in twelve years ago. I was about to ask you: What kind of nice thing you did twelve years ago?!"

The patient was flabbergasted by the surprise counterattack, his mind turned blank as he did not know how to answer the question.

The woman twisted her neck forcefully, threw several locks of hairs at her temper back to her head by throwing her head, then rushed to the front of the patient like an infuriated lioness, shouted:" How dare you to mention the thing happened twelve years ago! How dare you to mention the thing happened twelve years ago! You just think about it: Twelve years ago, what kind of nice thing you did?!"

"Hey! Well, what kind of nice thing have you done? I have not asked you yet; you want to ask me? Well! You just tell me what I did twelve years ago?" The patient had already calmed himself down, and forced himself to speak in a long drawl. The flame of his anger flashed up again by her domineering manner. But though his voice and tone was horrible, he still could not hide his diffidence.

The woman shrilled:"What you did? You killed my father! You seized his wealth by scheme! Twelve years ago, in the hostel what did you do? You just think about it! You tell me now!"

While gasping for air, she shouted, stampeded her feet on the carpet angrily and forcefully; among the pauses of her words, her sorrowful tears began to flow out of her red eyes and rushed down her cheeks like water rushing out of a breach in Yellow River(*Second longest river in China)!

Chapter 14 You—You All Remember, You Have Three Lives To Account For!

The unexpected eruption acted like an exploding grenade which was thrown into the room.

The doctor who remained in lazy fashion did not realize that a dust of his cigarette was shaken down onto his vest due to the explosion.

The crouching young man at the corner of the room was exhaling a breath which was barely noticeable to other people.

Particularly the patient began to fall into his dream with his widely opened eyes after he heard the unexpected words as if he had stood in front of the paper window twelve years ago again—for quite a while, after a long while, as if he had waken up from his nightmare, rattled:"What! You—you—you are the daughter of NinthOne Tao?—The—The..."

"I don't know NinthOne Tao or TenthOne Tao, I only know my father was called BrightSpring Kuang!" The woman stamped her feet forcibly on the carpet.

"Well, what! You are—you are the—the White..." the patient stammered out the words, could not continue his words though he wanted to.

His unfinished words made the woman erupt like an active volcano, began to erupt more violently, the eyes of the woman were emanating angry sparks, her voice began to act like a rattling machine gun, shrilled loudly:" White—White—What white? The sorcerer of White Lotus Society, right?" She laughed miserably once, said:"Humph! At this moment, you still want to put a wrong label on my father as a sorcerer of White Lotus Society! Just with you conscienceless words, you—you let my father's heart and liver be cut out while he was alive! You—You—" She began to sob sadly, said in a miserable voice:" Now, you just take your heart and liver out, let me see, what kind of heart do you have?!"

An emotion mixed with sorrow, anger, and hatred was turning every drop of the blood of the pitiable woman into a flame, which was uncontrollable! At the moment, if the sharp knife used in twelve years ago were at her hand, she would definitely pierce the knife into the chest of her cruel and sinister husband.

After her shrilling like a hurricane, her uncontrollable flame of anger began to cool down due to her tiredness, then she cried sorrowfully as if the sorrow could seep into the bones of everyone present. She stared at the patient angrily with a despising expression, thus began to tell her hair raising story.

"My goodness! My great manager!—" The woman suddenly called her husband in that unique way. " After you killed my father in that kind of fashion, do you know how you made our whole family look like? Do you want hear it now?" While sobbing, she said:" At that time, our whole family decided my father went to the town first and waited us there in order to avoid a disaster. Unexpectedly!" She stamped her feet down on the carpet again, said: "Unexpectedly, we could not see my father there in the town! We could only see a low mound of earth—that was a sad and lonely grave used to bury unknown person—with a heart-ripping wooden slip as only label!"

When she talked to here, her body began to tremble as if she caught a severe cold, her throat was choked by her sobbing! Due to the tremble and the choking, she really could not continue speak in a whole sentence, but she still tried to continue:"My goodness! My grandma, a woman near her seventy, when she saw the label, fainted to ground at once—in next day, she died in the town without any relative."

She sent a miserable laugh to the man who was transfixed, continued:"Now, you just count! Besides my poor father, one, two—two people lost their lives!"

The patient raised his eyes which sank into his eye sockets deeply with angry, shameful or hateful expression. He looked at other people first, then his wife who was in rage helplessly, as if he were begging: Please don't speak anymore. But his silent begging only increased the sorrow and rage of the woman! She tried hard to control her own emotion, continued bravely:" The most pitiable person was my mother! At that time, she rolled up and down over the mound, shouted to Heaven! The corners of her mouth were covered with bloody foams! The bloody foams, tears and mud made her face look like a ghost! A sharp stub of a little tree pierced into her ear for several centimeters, she even did not feel any pain! Well, what a horrible scene, less than half a year, she left us behind, went to other world! My goodness, she left to other world!"

The doctor who was leaning on the back of his chair began to take deep draw upon hearing the words, forgot that the flame of his cigarette had already extinguished for a long time.

Dry coughing sounds of 'um-hum-um-" which was sad began to spread out from the dim corner of the room from time to time.

At the moment, it was still bright outside, but inside the room, it was gloomy and dark as if the room had looked like one in a rain which had lasted for several days! The formless gloom made everyone feel like one basin of cold water was poured down from their heads! With that kind of horrible feeling, the woman whose face looked like a piece of white paper bent her fingers as if she were counting, while counting, she said in a miserable voice:"You—You all have to remember, those—those were three lives!"

She tried hard to continue:"My elder brother does not do well, though he does not put all his efforts, his temperament changed after the horrible experience, he aged for ten years at once. In a short while, white hairs began to show up on his head! How about me! Yes, how about myself—"

When she mentioned 'me', the horrible and sad past experience made her curl her mouth, she almost burst into laughter, said one word after another, one word for a breath while sobbing:" At that time, when I saw the hair-raising wooden label, I thought my father had already slept under the mound who died in that kind of miserable fashion! I only thought my sky was turned upside down! From then on, I became a fatherless girl, from then on, none would protect me anymore! From then on, I lost my most loved father!—I rushed to the body of my father, the mound—I thought nothing anymore! I only wanted to hug the body of my poor father—I tried very hard to excavate the earth, the mound of his grave!"

When she talked to here, she trembled to stretch her hands with the palms facing the ground; she waved her hands slowly from right to left; at the same time she looked around with her confused, sad and stiff pupils slowly as if she had wanted to show her hands to one thousand people in case they were in the room.

She shrilled loudly and sadly:"My goodness! You—You all have a look! You just look at my fingers!—"

The doctor watched her fingers carefully while listening to her sad words, though her fingernails were painted with pleasant nail polish, but if one looked carefully, it seemed that fingernails were not smooth and neat as the ones of other people, it seemed that the fingernails grew back after they were completely lost!

My goodness! That was the score for her excavating the mound of her father at that time!

At the moment the doctor felt as if some worms were wriggling on his skin. Then he listened calmly about the sad story of the woman:

"My goodness! I was only fifteen years old at that time. From then on within five years, almost my whole family was rooted out! I never dreamed that the whole family would disintegrate in that quick fashion—it happened much fast than a tornado—at that time I only had my elder brother left, we could only depend on each other. But my elder brother did not do anything good! As none could control him, thus he began to gamble and take opium, he would do anything as he liked. In a short time, he lost all our crop fields and wealth. When I was twenty years old, how pitiable it could be! I was deceived to Shanghai, I was sold to a brothel by my own brother!—"

"My cruel brother took all the money he got from selling me, from then on, he vanished for seven years! He recently came to me, thus we could see each other again."

The woman trembled, suddenly stretched her hands to cover her face! Then she put down her hands slowly again, sighed sadly, said:" My goodness, my fate was so horrible! In the fire pit, I was sneered, ridiculed, insulted, and tortured with an indelible memory! The Heaven offered me help! Fortunately within one year, I got married with someone. Yes, I would marry with someone!"

When she talked about 'the marry with someone', she suddenly raised her extremely gloomy eyes, as if a swallow skipped onto the surface of a water, she cast a miserable glance on the young man in the room who was with a pale face like a piece of white paper, her passionate gaze made the pale face recover a strange redness at once.

At the moment the young man wore an extremely painful expression on his face, the expression just looked like a man who was watching his beloved rose was being destroyed by a thunderstorm and he could not do anything about that. The doctor took down the cigarette which had already extinguished for a long time at the corner of his mouth, nodded his head silently. He was thinking:" Well! A toxic arrow of recalling broke a heart, at the same time the metal arrowhead wounded another heart!"

Then the woman stared at the patient with her vicious looking once, raised her head, howled despairingly: " My—My goodness! I—how could I expect! I have married a man who killed my father and I would never live with him under same sky!"

The pitiful woman finished her last sentence, at the same time, she used up all her energy. She looked like a person who just recovered her illness, ran for several miles with one breath. She stretched her hands to touch head head, tottered, as if the floor of the room had became the deck of a ship floating on an ocean.

"My—goodness!" At the moment a very low shouting voice which sounded as if a mosquito or fly were buzzing blurted out by Little Qiu. He wanted to rush forward to support the tottering woman. But when he looked at the cold gaze across him, he suddenly came into reality, thus stopped his action, even his preparatory action stopped at once as if someone slammed hard on a brake, thus he did not show any sign on his manner.

It seemed the woman was hypnotized at the moment by some invisible hand when Little Qiu was trying and stopping his action, she staggered several steps, rushed toward the chest of Little Qiu like a drunkard, in the end she plopped down into a chair at his side.

Chapter 15 Now, It's My Turn To Treat You In Same Fashion

Based on the tiny movements and signs, it seemed there was a hiding current of feeling flowing around in imperceptible fashion, which could ignite hot spark. The calm doctor observed the feeling very clearly. At the moment there was another opinion entering his calm mind. He thought:" Based on my observation, it seems the young man and woman have established some kind of relationship for a long time; maybe before she married with BrilliantTalent Wang, they had already developed some kind of feeling to each other."

He developed the opinion when he noticed the unique expression of the woman when she mentioned the words 'marry with someone'.

At the moment, he thought in that fashion, took out his lighter, relighted the half cigarette reservedly, due to his reserve, his forehead began to pile up a downhearted shadow, But the shadow just lingered for a moment, he leaned his back more closely on the chair, closed his eyes, sent his thinking into the ocean of deep reasoning.

He thought at the beginning in such fashion:" For all the things, it could be summarized as following: 'This BrilliantTalent Wang killed a person with an evil and sinister method twelve years ago. Five years later he got married with the girl of the murdered.

Another seven years passed, he came across the son of the murdered—the brother of his wife whom he never met before—he mistook the brother as the ghost of the murdered twelve years ago. He became extremely panicked, divulged the incident to his wife. Then she got to know he was the one who got her father killed, thus she colluded with her brother and another person, with various horrible methods, carried out the planned intimidation. Thus, various strange and weird things happened.' This should be the outline of the whole incident—"

He then thought:" Among all the facts, there are several points needed to pay attention. First, the son of the murdered showed up in front of BrilliantTalent Wang without any ill intention, which happened coincidentally, till the third time when the ghost showed up again, it became a planned action;

Second, the director of the whole thing is Little Qiu, the one who takes opium definitely could not come up with such a meticulous plan, he is just an actor;

Third, the one who acted like a ghost, could his appearance look exactly like his father who died twelve years ago? Which depended upon the abnormal reaction of the observer: Based on genetics, father and son look similar in appearance to some extent, which is quite common, thus nothing is strange about that. As to no difference at all, which is definitely not true. No matter how deep the image left in one's memory, after twelve years, the image would definitely become murky, just like the film of a photograph, after while, it would deteriorate to some extent. Nevertheless, as the image is kept in one's memory for so many years, if one bumps an image which looks similar, then the image will easily cause a psychological illusion, thus the similarity for one part becomes three parts, three parts become nine or ten parts. The thing BrilliantTalent Wang bumped should happen in such a way;

Fourth, how the actor dressed up like the real one in that kind of vivid fashion in the play? The question was easy to give an answer, because the actor witnessed the clothes of his father when he escaped from the home, thus he definitely had the impression. Twelve years later, it would not be difficult for him to dress up like his father. As to the steel-fork-like wrinkles between his eyebrows and the black mole on the ear, it was just a piece of cake;

Fifth, among the bunch—PendantJade, Little QIu and the one who takes opium—why they want to intimidate the well-known person in that kind of fashion? Avenge for her father, let the sinister and evil person be tortured mentally, which should be the motive of PendantJade? But the punitive methods might be from Little Qiu—furthermore, Little Qiu needs some money badly, maybe that could be taken as one of the reasons, but the reason might not be reliable, maybe it was just used a smoke screen. Besides the two motives above, there should be another hiding motive. Maybe hiding motive is to snatch something away out of the chaos, which should be the motive of Little Qiu. As to whether the woman could understand the hiding motive, it still needs to be confirmed."

"In a summary..." Several wisps of smokes came out of the corners of his mouth, he wanted to continue his thinking. But at the moment, his calm thinking was interrupted by a very loud shouting. He heard the patient began to shout at his side as if he went crazy:" Well, well, well! Wonderful! You—you bunch of ghosts! One wants to avenge her father as a filial daughter! One acts as a hero to uphold justice! Still another one—another one—well! You nearly frightened me to death, what do you want to do with me? Well! Wonderful! It seems that you want to get out of something! You just exchange silent glances at each other, do you think I don't know forever?"

He paused his angry and evil voice for a moment, then said through his clenched teeth:"Wonderful! As you have already tried to harm me, now it's my turn to treat you in same fashion! Humph!"

The bombing voice made the doctor open his tired eyes. He was shocked by what he was watching!

He was not sure what was the cause of this second huge fire? In fact, the rage was much more stronger than before, the rage was induced by the sparks in the eyes of the young man and woman.

The patient had already stood up from the chair, supported by his thick cane, was trembling uncontrollably; his anger was really ignited, became a hot flame, then sublimated into a hot vapor. What more horrible was his sleepy face!

Dear Readers, had you seen the quarrel among the ferocious ghosts in hell? Certainly you had not. Then, you just watched the expression of BrilliantTalent Wang, at least his expression was equal to the expression of a ferocious ghost in hell!

His pale face turned livid due to his rage; the livid face was covered by an oily film; there were many dark spots under the oily livid face—once a doctor surveyed the spots surprisingly for several seconds—his teeth was protruding froward, his eyes sank deeply into his sockets—no matter who saw the eye sockets, one might associate them with the ones one saw in the skeleton of a museum! For the skeleton, there were no eyes in it, but his sockets were with a pair of shiny things in them, sparkling! Therefore, it was much horrible than the skeleton!

At the moment it seemed he acted like a snake crawling out its den after it was being disturbed. He raised the cane in his trembling hand, adopted a posture as if he wanted to rush forward at any moment, which looked just like the tongue of the snake. The hateful gaze was staring PendantJade for a while, then Little Qiu for a while in slowly alternate fashion. He was thinking which of his enemies should be attacked first? At the same time it seemed that he was deciding which critical part of his enemy should be squirted with his venom violently!

His expression was horrible, his two potential targets were trembling due to the gaze, each of them could only huddle together by himself/herself due to fright, even the calm doctor sensed something wrong all over his body.

At the moment if nothing else happened, nothing came forward to prevent his action, maybe in one minute, something horrible might happen in the room.

But the prevention did happen, thus the horrible thing was prevented to occur in the room.

"Well, just slow down a bit! There is still one important thing needed to be solved," the doctor said in an extremely cold voice.

"What thing?!" the strange voice of the doctor made the patient turn his head angrily with his ferocious looking, asked loudly, but based on his tone, he did not care anymore about the warning of the 'explosive break' of his blood vessel.

"How about you have a seat to listen?" the doctor drew a circle in air with his unlighted cigarette as his custom, said calmly and leisurely. "There is an urgent problem needed to be solved, which is related to your life and reputation."

"About my life and reputation?" A puzzling expression showed up in his angry eyes. He was really obedient! Just like a well trained pug, he sat down in the chair haltingly.

"Last night, Dr. Xia told me: He lost something in this place," the doctor said in his usual neither warm nor cold tone.

"Do I need to pay for the thing he lost in my place?" the patient said in an angry voice. His nostrils distended once.

"I hope you will not shoulder the responsibility to pay the thing lost, it is much better for you," the doctor said coldly.

"What was the thing he lost?" the patient asked in a fretful voice.

"It is a little tube with the extract of nux vomica—merely a little tube."

"What the extract for?" the patient asked with a weird voice.

"A poison!" the doctor said loudly and curtly.

An apprehensive expression showed up in the eyes of the patient, at the same time, the young man and woman showed similar expression on their faces!

The doctor continued:"Though it is just a small tube, the amount is enough to kill ten pigs!" While speaking, suddenly he looked at Little Qiu with an extremely tense expression, shouted sternly:" Mr. Qiu, what was the white powder you poured into the milk cup a while ago?"

It seemed that Little Qiu was stricken by a lightning accidentally, his frightening eyes nearly jumped out of his eye sockets.

The woman understood the meaning of the unexpected words, while gasping, she stared at Little Qiu with a surprising expression.

There were total eight eyes in the room, and six of them were staring at the young man who was staying in the dim corner of the room at once.

At the tense moment, another horrible thing happened in the room!

At the moment pea-size sweat drops were rushing out his forehead profusely. He supported all his weight on his cane. At the moment, he trembled violently to stand up, but at once plopped down into the chair powerlessly. He tried with all his efforts to stare at Little Qiu angrily and frighteningly, the expression in his eyes could not be described with words. He uttered several words among his heavy gasping:"Little ... Little Qiu, you ... you are a ghost! You ... You ...You dare—You... dare..."

He wanted to say:"You dare to use poison to kill me!" But he did not finish the sentence. When he was half a way through, he stretched his hands to catch his throat, as if there were a fire inside his throat, then he caught the black brocade chest of his night gown, it seemed that he was in extremely excruciating pain! In the short moment! Horrible! He took back his gaze from Little Qiu suddenly, it seemed that his gaze was called back by a voice—he did not look at Little Qiu, PendantJade and the doctor. He raised his trembling eyes, it seemed that he was searching for another person in the room who did not exist, it seemed that his horrible expression demonstrated that another person coming into the room! He begged in a bewitched voice, shouted gloomily and sadly in an incoherent way:"My goodness! You—you—you let me—confess—"

Before he could finish his words, they could hear the rumbling sounds within his throat as if a train just started to move! Within several seconds, they noticed his pupils starting to expand, become confused, then fixed without a bit movement! In the end, he stretched his hand, caught wildly in air, then his body fell into a period of spasm! Then they heard a plopping sound, his cane of oak wood fell down from his another hand onto the exquisite carpet.

Then, everything fell into silence.

Chapter 16 I Invite You To Test A 'Tasty' Dying Method!

Dear readers, you might ask:"What's wrong?"

I could tell you:"It seems that our well-known person, in a very short time, mustered all his energy to his running legs, dashed forward to reach the destination of the finish line of the 'marathon'!"

At the moment, the doctor was at the side the runner of the marathon. In theory, the doctor should be shocked or at least surprised when he saw the patient was running at that kind of speed, but it seemed that he did not show any bit of surprise on his calm face; he acted as if he had known the thing would happen fifty years ago.

He really acted easily and casually.

You see, he stubbed out the cigarette in his hand solemnly, put it back into his exquisite pack carefully, as if he wanted to say: To him, the value of the well-known person was less than that of the half cigarette in his hand!

After he put back the the half cigarette, he jumped up agilely, went to the door, checked whether the door was bolted well.

Then he turned, went to the side of the well-known person who was calm and patient at the moment, bent his body, touched the forehead of the person, then opened the noble eyelids of the well-known person which despised everybody when he was alive, checked for a moment, then turned his body, kicked the cane on the carpet, picked it up calmly, put it back at the side of its owner, then turned back, said calmly to the young man and woman who acted as if there were just shocked by an electricity a moment ago:"Well, well, a cadelle fell into a cooking pot, it is cooked already!"

The young man and woman stared their eyes widely open and uttered no sound as if they were a pair of ice sculptures.

The woman exhaled heavily as if a child fell down heavily on ground after quite a while. She was panic, acted haltingly to go forward to check the man who had murdered her beloved father carefully. But she was stopped by the merciful doctor, the doctor said:" There is no value to visit. For such a kind of disgusting things, you have already come across a lot in roads for recent years."

"Really! He ... He... was he dead?" The tongue of the woman was dancing as if trills were coming out of her mouth. It seemed that she just woke up from her dream.

"Yes! It seems..." the doctor said. "He could not live anymore." What! It was really unintelligible to know a woman! Three minutes ago, to her, the well-known person was a man who killed her father and they could not live under one sky. But, three minutes later, at least she did not take him as the one who could not live under one sky as he killed her father. Therefore, her eyes which had not dried yet became reddish again, she raised her painful, fearful, trembling and conflicting eyes, glanced first at the chair the man sat a minute ago, then at the door, in the end stared at Little Qiu, asked in a reprimanding voice:"You—you—you—"

She wanted to say:"How could you do that kind of thing? What should we do now?"

"You need not to worry! Nobody will come into this room for the time being. I will take care of everything," the doctor looked at the door while saying the comforting words.

It seemed the reply of the doctor gave an opportunity for the young man to get back his soul, he noticed the reprimanding gaze of the young woman, said in a crying tone while putting much efforts:"Well! Pendant—Well! Mrs. Wang! I did not—no—I really did not—"

It seemed that a blockade line was set up in his throat, and there was an impenetrable iron fence at the tip of his tongue.

The doctor looked at the pitiable man as if he had lost his soul with a compassionate expression at the corners of his eyes, then turned to look at the corpse who was with angry and horrible expression, his eyes turned around once.

"Ha Ha Ha Ha Ha!" he raised his head and began to laugh weirdly as if he were an owl crying in night.

The laughter threw the young man and woman into a heavy fog.

The doctor went forward, patted the shoulder of Little Qiu, as if a father were offering comfort to a child who had been scolded.

"My good brother! You need not to be haste!" he said. "I know you have not stolen the toxin of Dr. Xia, furthermore, you did not put anything into the milk. In another words, Dr. Xia did not lose any his nux vomica or the extract of nux vomica, that means you did not poison your master to death!"

He paused a bit, then added resolutely:" Yes, I have to admit that what I said a moment ago was just joking words, you needn't to mind my words at all."

"Joke?!" Little Qiu said in his trembling voice, it seemed that he became completely confused.

"What! You mean he did not poison him to death? He—he did not poison him to death! Is it true?" The woman interrupted hurriedly. In her apprehensive eyes, there was a bit pleasant hope, but there was an obvious disbelief in her tone.

"Why should I deceive you?" the doctor said earnestly and resolutely.

"Well, then why he died?" She looked at the stiff corpse on the carpet apprehensively and bewilderingly.

"I am doing a kind of experiment..." It seemed that doctor was caring about the half cigarette, he took out his pack slowly from his pocket. He continued:"If you are not hungry, do you want to listen my experimental method?"

Little Qiu became even more confused.

The more she listened, the more the apprehensive woman could not understand.

The doctor waved his hand to them as if he were greeting his guests, said:"Just sit down for a moment, okay?"

They had already realized it was not easy to act against the order of the legendary man. They could only follow his order helplessly and obediently.

Though they sat down in the sofas, it seemed that they were sitting on a hot stove, their attentions were drawn to the corpse; every passing second could only increase their apprehension and anxiety. It seemed their hands and feet became redundant, they did not know where to put them.

The doctor sat in his chair, said after he breathed several calm circles of smoke from his mouth:"I think you both should not focus your attention on the disgusting thing, you should think more broadly, the more broad the better; as to the corpse, the smaller, the better. You should take the corpse as a dead fly! If you think in such a way, it might be good to your body and health."

Though the doctor said the words lightly as if the thing mattered nothing at all. In fact, there was a horrible corpse lying in front of them! The corpse definitely could not change into a size of a fly by his words. Thus, his words still could not change the anxious and uncomfortable manner of the young man and woman.

He looked at them, it seemed that he became a bit impatient, thus he said in a serious tone with a long face:"Yes, you should adopt the philosophy of the dead man! Well, you just think about it: Twelve years ago, he witnessed that the heart and liver were cut out of a man alive, he even did not frown a bit! Which is a calm attitude one must adopt when one wants to get rich! Could not you learn from him?"

The words took some effect. There were a gloomy and desolate shadow showed up on the pale face of the woman. As expected, she took her eyes back from the corpse, and stared at the fingernails which had been used to excavate the mound. Upon hearing the words, the young man seemed to recall the cruelty and evilness of the man when he was alive, the color of his face changed at once! It seemed that his courage was boosted up again.

The doctor smiled to them, said:"Very well, then you just listen my story."

"In a foreign country, there was a well-known psychologist..." he took a deep draw, shook the toe cap of his leather shoe while saying.

Well, he was really wonderful! Under such a kind of situation, how could he have a mood to talk about that kind of thing! Furthermore, he talked about a foreign psychologist, did it have anything to do with the current situation?

They looked at the door and him apprehensively. They sensed their stomachs were a bit itchy, heard he said in a calm voice:" The psychologist told people: He would not use a knife, a gun, or anything which could be used to kill a person, he needs only a magical method to send a person to the 'complete rest'."

"Once, he was permitted by authority to do his test on a condemned person. He said humorously to the condemned person:" 'Eating' and 'dying' are two important problems for a human. For eating, one has to choose tasty foods; for dying, one certainly has to choose a 'tasty' method. It is too bitter to be hung, it is too spicy to be electrocuted, therefore I want to ask you to try a tasty method to die."

"He—the psychologist—used a square piece of cloth, wrapped the eyes of the condemned tightly, then took the condemned to a side of a faucet, said: 'Now I will cut your blood vessels to bleed all your blood out, thus you will die painlessly.' While talking, he used a knife cut the blood vessels of the condemned for a while with force—you have to remember, he used the back of the knife—then he turned on the faucet slightly, let the water flow down one drop after another. He said:'Your blood vessels have already been severed! Have you heard the sound? Your blood is flowing out! Have you felt any pain? At the moment, you have already lost about thirty per cent of your blood! Well, fifty per cent! Seventy per cent! Well! Only twenty per cent left! Only ten per cent left! Well! It almost completely comes out! Well, your blood is completely bled out! You will die now! You see, isn't it painless?'—"

"The psychologist repeated three times about the 'painless', then he noticed the condemned dropping his head down gradually. When he took down the square cloth from the face of the condemned, as expected the condemned had already passed away and went to Heaven!"

The doctor finished his story in a breath eloquently, then he began to burst into laughter, then explained:" Though it seems the story was absurd, I only heard the story from another person. Thus I did not believe the words, I wanted to give a try. I have to thank Mr. Wang who was generous and offered an opportunity to increase my knowledge!"

The young man became entranced to the story. When the story came to the end, it seemed that he still was confused. Then after further thinking, it seemed that he was enlightened suddenly, he shouted:" Well! You copied the method of the psychologist! You—"

"You are right. My words were equal in meaning to the words the psychologist told to the condemned one," the doctor echoed with a smile.

The young man said expectantly:"He—he was frightened to death by you."

The doctor nodded his head, said:"Yes, I frightened him to death and saved you both."

"Have you saved us? But you have already ruined us." The young man looked at the corpse with a nervous expression.

"Have I ruined you? I have to remind you, please remember: Dr. Xia has already said the dead one has a very serious heart problem, furthermore, I am a doctor, I still can talk with my tongue." The doctor stood up, flipped the butt of his tenth cigarette into the spittoon lightly. He added in a comforting tone:"I have to ask you 'restrain your grief and face the unexpected change', first you eat something for your lunch, then boost yourselves up to prepare for the grand funeral thing—"

Then he turned his gaze to the new widow who became the widow a moment ago, said:"Well, Mrs. Wang. Well, no! For the moment let me call you Ms. Kuang, I hope in near future, I could call you the sweetheart of Mr Qiu. Well, Ms. Kuang, I wish you both could jointly drink a cup of hot coffee in the bustling funeral room!"

The pale face of the woman turned crimson, she did not have time to look at the corpse, only tidied her clothes a bit subconsciously.

Little Qiu controlled his anger, said nervously:"But, I have to remind you, you should remember: It's a human life!"

"Human life?!" the doctor turned his head suddenly, and said. "In this lovely world at the moment, the most worthless words are the two words. You need not worry about that, you just relax, leave everything to me!"

When he mentioned 'me', he did not point his finger at his nose but his ear.

Chapter 17 A Last Little Episode Which Had Not Been Told Yet!

When the story came to here, the story should come to an end as it had already used several hundred exclamation mark '!'. But at the point of the tired pen of the author, it seemed that there was still something needed to be added:

In the day, Dr. ShadowChange Yu came out of the resting room, he first turned the floor type radio on to let it broadcast its normal program, then went to the outside to tell the servants:" Mr. Wang had a sudden attack, before I could inject a heart stimulant, he had already passed away!" Though the servants were surprised by the news, they knew for the time being the host wore an emaciated and abnormal expression, had already prepared for the day, thus they were not extremely shocked by the news.

After Dr. Yu left, Dr. Xia was the first one arrived at the scene. The old doctor checked the dead body, then he knit his eyebrows tightly, in the end, he said:" The host died of a sudden heart attack, which could not be salvaged by any medical treatment." As the death was confirmed by two 'reliable' people with a consensus. Thus, the thing did not cause any trouble at that time, furthermore, it did not cause any problem from then on.

After our well-known person died, his only legal heir—his wife, PendantJade—took all the property. Well, well, if one just thought it further, it certainly contained the karma, furthermore, the karma was so natural, it did not contain any superstitious component.

The woman had a merciful heart. She forgave her elder brother—AnotherSpring Kuang. She was generous, she gave a little part of her wealth to her elder brother willingly—to her, she thought the wealth of BrilliantTalent Wang was inherited from her father; as it was her father's wealth, it was quite reasonable to give some to him.

But for a man who was addicted to opium, what did it mean to own a lot of wealth suddenly? It was not hard to imagine the result. In a short time, he became a real ghost from an actor playing as a ghost. He lost his interest to have a job, was only interested in his old job, and worked very seriously about his old job, thus became a real ghost.

As to whether MiddleHero Qiu, after the incident, would get married with PendantJade, I really did not know. As when I started to write the story, I just wanted to tell something about 'my friend' and did not want to write a story about relationship between a man and a woman, thus I was not responsible to report the outcome of their relationship here.

In the end, I had to talk something about 'my friend', the miraculous Dr. ShadowChange Yu, what did he get out of the thing?

As I mentioned Dr. Yu—of course, he had many other names and professions—always held his principle ' to get something out of a thing', he often used the slogan:" Thing is thing, business is business." This time though he acted as an assistant of a doctor, but in the play, he had already gotten some habit of a famous doctor, in his temporary booklet for his case diagnosis, he jotted nothing for his profit as if the patient were so poor that he could not pay any money for the diagnosis and treatment. That he jotted down nothing did not mean he did not charge a single penny for his service... Furthermore, he came across a wealthy famous person.

Thus, when he left the house in the day, twenty thousand dollars were already put into his black bag with a bit courtesy as his fee for his diagnosis and treatment of the patient—No! It should be taken as a hushing money, or the pay for killing someone—just like IntelligentOne Wang got his pay for killing someone twelve years ago.

Mr. Time never cared about the mysterious and weird things happened and happening in the world, he only rushed forward without looking around for anything. In a blink, our famous well-known person had already died for one hundred days.

In the day, Mrs. Wang took her time coming to a famous Buddhist temple, asked the monks to pray for her dead husband to let him go to Heaven as a usual practice. At one corner of the temple with a lot of tall trees, Mrs. Wang was playing her role as usual; Mr. Qiu was taking care of everything as usual; the monks were acting as usual to pray for the dead soul of IntelligentOne Wang to let him go into the heaven reserved specially for evil people.

What a coincidence! The author wanted to borrow a sentence for ancient novelists:'Everything happens by coincidence!' In the day, in another corner of the temple, in a grand praying hall—the monk, SnowyNature, who first appeared in the story, was invited to talk about Buddhism in the hall; in his speech, he still repeated the words he said before:

If an individual kills a man, then the individual could not escape the fate he will be killed by other people!

Unfortunately Master SnowyNature did not know anything about the well-known person in our story, otherwise, he maybe added several more words:

If an individual seizes someone's wealth by a scheme, then the wealth of the individual could not escape the fate that it would be seized by other people!

What a coincidence! In the day, Dr. ShadowChange Yu was among the men who were listening to the lecture. How could he come to the lecture? It was really funny for his reason to show up in the lecture. After he got the bloody money for his diagnosis and treatment in the house of the well-known person, in a short while he got his payback of being dumped by his girlfriend miserably. In the first place, he believed Buddhism to some extent, though not wholeheartedly. Usually he did not like to listen to the lecture about Buddhism, but this time due to his being dumped, he came to the temple, stayed for about five minutes in the lecture. To him, it should be taken as a repentance for his sin?

As to repentance, he killed the well-known person in that kind of weird method, shouldn't he repent?

No! He needed not to repent, there was another person who needed to repent in the story, the last person, we still had not come to the little episode yet.

After BrilliantTalent Wang passed away, Dr. Yu opened his eyelids to check. Well! How could it be so strange! At the moment he noticed the person died of poison! Due to some reason, he did not speak out the thing, rather he released a smoke screen to cover up the real cause.

Who was the murderer? It was needless to say, he was Little Qiu.

But what kind of thing Little Qiu used to poison his teacher to death?

Based on the analysis of Dr. Yu: He must use some chronic poison which was not easy to notice, for many days, he gave the poison gradually to his teacher.

Then, did he put the poison in the day when he prepared the milk? Well, certainly not, definitely not. You just think about it: How dare a murderer to add a poison in front of a doctor? There was no such a kind of fool in the world.

Then why Dr. Xia did not say anything about the death in the day? Yes, he had the ability to notice the signs of poisoning, how could he not notice the signs? Definitely he could not be worse in his ability than the novice who just entered the medical field? Well! It was just a joke!

But there were something hiding in the joke.

In the first place, when Dr. Xia noticed the expression of the patient, he immediately sensed something was wrong, based on the sign the patient showed up at the last moment of his life, the patient had a tonic spasm—which was called opisthotonos by doctors of Chinese Medicine—which was a sign for poisoning. When he thought about poisoning, he immediately remembered that he talked about the extract of nux vomica to the mysterious doctor. Well, my goodness! Did the guy listen to his words and let the patient swallow a lot of more the extract than necessary? It seemed that the thing was true, due to the overdose of the extract, the patient died in such a kind of way. If the patient died in such fashion, then he had to shoulder some indirect responsibility! The reliable old doctor was a timid person in first place. When he figured out the the reason, he immediately kept his mouth shut tightly as if he had sealed his mouth tightly with his medical tape in a criss-cross fashion.

Well, the only person who got bad result was BrilliantTalent Wang, the person who benefited most was Little Qiu. You just think about it, the thing is very funny.

Then why Little Qiu wanted to poison his well-known teacher to death? Of course the thing was involved a sad romantic story. If dear readers could keep the secret, I would like to tell you about it secretly.

In the first place, PendantJade met Mr. Qiu before BrilliantTalent Wang as expected by Dr. Yu. They came across each other in the so-called fire pit—of course at that time she had a nickname which should be shiny like eon light—at the time, they swore to each other for their marriage. But my dear readers, have you seen the Cupid's Arrow? Well, don't you see the little arrow is made of pure gold? Thus, with sure result, Little Qiu was a loser for the love affair. At that time, the passionate young man nearly killed himself for the thing, he nearly lost his mind. At last, he found a solution as he had no other options: He heard about his rival in love, a rich businessman in the city, whom he did not meet before. Thus he asked around, through his efforts, he became a disciple of his, thus he could access 'the origin of his life.'

The poor guy, he really tried very hard.

Thus once when he heard about the cruel incident of his master from PendantJade, with his passionate fire which ignited a flame of an uncontrollable 'justice feeling' in his heart, he made up his mind resolutely to avenge her father's death, thus he could get his idol completely out of the unreasonable environment.

Then could his brave action be taken as an upright one completely? About the thing, the author could not give a definite answer for the time being.

Nevertheless, dear readers, you just think about it: Even in the shiny gold beach, no matter how sparkling the gold sands look, could they just be pure golds without a bit sand?

Besides, there was another thought: Maybe BrilliantTalent Wang began to suspect Little Qiu for the ghost play; thus Little Qiu could not do anything but poison him. That should be another possible reason.

When we talked about the miraculous person, some readers had already gotten to know his character: For his life, he did a lot of 'bad things with good intention' or 'good things with bad intention', but what he hated most was murder and blood—he was quite different with the famous and momentary Hitler—he never killed anyone, thus he needed not to repent.

But upon further thinking, he still needed to do his repentance. In theory, in this incident, he knew the real killer, thus he should let the killer face the justice.

Then why he did not speak out?

According to laws of the human world, he committed 'a crime of shielding'—In jurisprudence, it is called 'a crime of omission'—to Buddhism, his misdemeanor is called sharing the crime, which is nearly equal to the original crime. But in mind of the miraculous person, he held a tenet. Let me take this opportunity to tell you: He think no matter what kind of person, so long as he commits a crime under his passionate love, then the crime is forgivable. Due to his weird tenet, thus he did not expose the kill done by Little Qiu. He not only did not expose the crime but also tried to cover up with a smokescreen.

These are all the mysteries of this weird incident.

Dear readers, do you think the miraculous friend should repent for his evil thinking or not?

Did you love *Walking Bloody Paper Dolls*? Then you should read *Fortunes of Officials*[1] by Renfu Xiao!

Fortunes of Officials is a story about the whole process of StrongIdeal Gao to become the most powerful person-- the secretary from deputy secretary of municipal committee of Near Violet City with a population of seven million people and to resign from the post. Like other place, Near Violet was filled opportunities, restlessness and uneasiness in the transformation period. As the most powerful person in the city, StrongIdeal Gao had to face various enticements and schemes and sufferings, but he withstood various challenges, took the great opportunities of the

---

1. https://books2read.com/u/mqqa7v

2. https://books2read.com/u/mqqa7v

Reform and Opening Door Policy, and made a great contribution to the economic development of the city under the tenet: As the most powerful person in the place, local people must benefit from his performance, thus he was well loved by the people of the city.

About the Author

LiaoHong Sun was a famous detective writer in 1930s and an important writer in the modern history of detective literacy in China. His grandfather opened a clock shop in Shanghai, his father was good at painting in Chinese style, among of the three brothers, he inherited the painting skill of his father. He usually did not care about his outer appearance, though he was not rich, he was ready to help other people so long as they came to him, did not leave any manuscript to the world. At the beginning he wrote about everything, would write on anything in his home such as calendars and the back of the cigarette packs so long as he could, and became an editor-in-chief for *Great Detective* in 1946. He published many detective novels such as *Ghost Hand*, *Blue Rattle Snake*, *A Legendary Story of A Chivalrous Thief*, *Walking Bloody Paper Dolls*, *Green Candle Light* etc. and translated some foreign novels into Chinese. At the beginning of 1950s, he wrote several plays such as *Long Lasting Loyalty*, *Three Unwillingness*, *Unjustly Banished Immortal* etc.

www.ingramcontent.com/pod-product-compliance
Lightning Source LLC
Chambersburg PA
CBHW021228130726
47988CB00002B/877